The Foot of Our Stairs

Daddy's Kite

Rabbit Rabbit

Angels

Calendar Girl

A Light in Time

Sweet William

Nineteen Eighty-Five

Wishes

Argent

Lessons

Seeing is Believing

Shopping List

Acting Out

Doors

Wedding Cake

And God Laughed

The Foot of Our Stairs

Well, I'll go to the foot of our stairs. Such an odd thing to say. For those of us who frequent obscure Internet pages in the same way a compulsive eater grazes the tables at a buffet, it is, apparently, a phrase that can give rise to many interesting conjectures. I've been told it's regarded as a Northern expression. Well, I spent several years in the north and never heard it uttered. But in the south I've often heard it. It's a colourful way to express incredulity. It's the equivalent of Victor Meldrew not believing it. An alternative to being a monkey's uncle. Or being blowed or jiggered. Or something ruder. I think that everyone has a foot of their stairs, even if they live in a ground-floor flat, or a bungalow that has yet to scale the dizzy heights of chalet-dom.

The foot of our stairs is where I find myself when things come at me from an unexpected direction because that is where I stood as a child, gazing up at a flight of steep narrow stairs that led, as I knew full well, to a place where scary but unseen beings lived. If you stood still and held your breath you could catch the faintest whisper of movement and sense the draught from something shifting, coiling and uncoiling, lying in wait. In the gloom above, darker shapes stirred. I dreaded having to climb these stairs alone, but even when my mother had asked Big Sister to help me by switching on the light in the hall, most times the request was ignored and I was left to face the problem on my own. I had a solution, of sorts. The middle of the stairs was covered by a thin strip of dusty carpet, held tight by iron stair rods. This carpet was wearing thin under the daily assault of family life but somewhere in the fading colours were pale pink flowers and mossy green leaves. To one side a simple cylindrical hand rail was fastened to the wall. Three brackets held it: top, bottom and middle. This meant you could grip the rail at the top, swing your feet up to the side, resting them on the narrowest of skirting boards, and slide down the rail to the foot of the stairs at what seemed a very great speed. Apart from the bit in the middle, of course, where there would be a swift pause to re-position hands. It entailed a bruising contact with the middle bracket, but that was a small price to pay for not being caught by the Terrors who lived at the top Sometimes I would just throw myself down if it all got too much.

Having been told for the umpteenth time that I was old enough to go to the bathroom by myself, I would brave the stairs in the dark and rush into the room at the top, switching on the light with a gasp of relief. This switch was much lower than the ones in the hallway, and on tiptoes I could just about manage to reach. Coming back down was where my nerve usually broke. The light had to be turned out, leaving a terrifying, dark gap between the bathroom doorway, where I was safe, and the light coming from the living-room down below. If I couldn't rush across that gap and swing up onto the handrail fast enough then a deliberate fall to the bottom was my best bet. Bruises didn't matter as long as I arrived at the foot of the stairs.

This whole 'getting to the foot of the stairs' problem lasted for all of the time between 'you're old enough to go upstairs on your own' and actually being tall enough to reach the light switches in the hall, though I was *never* tall enough that I could feel comfortable being upstairs alone at night. There was something in the area of the upstairs landing. Something I could feel .pressing close around me and making my heart beat faster. Something that watched me.

So, for me, the foot of our stairs is a very real place. It's a place of relative safety from which I can contemplate the strange things lurking at the top without actually going there myself. It gives a bit of distance between normal life and the weird stuff.

Welcome to the foot of our stairs. Enjoy the weird stuff. Stay safe.

Daddy's Kite

Mel rolled over and into the welcoming embrace of the slight dip in the middle of the bed. She could feel by the way the mattress gave that the bed was all hers. She stretched out and luxuriated in the space and warmth. It wasn't like Jamie to get up before her, especially on a cold, dark morning. Winter was coming on apace and, until the central heating clicked on for its morning burst, the house was a little too chilly first thing for his liking. He preferred to wait for Mel to get up and start the coffee, knowing that by the time the smell had wafted as far as the bedroom, the house would have begun to warm up. And still it took a few calls from Mel up the stairs to rouse him properly. It wasn't the same for her. Since having the children Mel's sleep patterns had changed so much she never bothered setting an alarm knowing that at the usual time – whether in winter's cold dark or the bird-song frenzy of a summer morning – she'd be wide awake and ready to go. She lay there listening for sounds of life from the kitchen but it all seemed suspiciously quiet downstairs. Maybe Jamie was sneaking around, trying not to disturb her or the girls. He'd had a lot of work worry lately. Perhaps that was why he was up early. It also accounted for the grumpiness at home. She and the girls had been almost tiptoeing around him for weeks but whenever she asked if he was OK he'd mutter something about having a headache and needing some peace to think. Only yesterday morning five-year-old Mia had asked when Daddy was going to start playing again. 'He's a bit busy thinking about work stuff at the moment,' she'd explained, 'but Mummy can still play with you.' A world-weary sigh had issued from Isabella, two years Mia's senior. 'But Mum, you don't think of the *good* games like Daddy.' It was true, Mel reflected, Jamie had an amazing imagination. He could paint the most wonderful word-pictures for the three of them and before they knew what was happening all of them would be roped into one of his fantasy adventures. She giggled to herself as she remembered the Roman Chariot Race in the middle of the supermarket when Mia was just toddling. The looks on people's faces! You'd think they'd be grateful to have someone break up the tedium of yet another shopping trip.

Finally Mel decided that she'd better get up, knowing that Jamie would never find which cupboards things were kept in. She pictured the mess he could create in her beautifully-organised kitchen and shuddered. Yawning and pulling her dressing-gown around her she shuffled towards the bathroom. No lights were on and the house seemed deserted so she almost screamed when she pushed the door open and saw something crouched in the dark. She had reached for the light-pull automatically and, as the room was flooded with harsh light, she realised it was Jamie. He was huddled on the floor, against the bath panel, his arms wrapped around himself. His body was shaking with huge sobs that he was trying to muffle in his hunched over body.

'Jamie! Whatever...'

She stopped, got down on the floor beside her husband and wrapped her arms around him.

It seemed to take an eternity for him to calm down. She rocked him and murmured wordless noises against his hair as though he were one of the girls, after some upset or fall. Slowly he pulled himself together but held onto her as if she were a lifeline. He looked terrible. His reddened eyes and blotchy face were new to Mel and she realised she had never seen him cry before. She put her hands gently to each side of his face and held his gaze. 'Jamie….whatever it is, absolutely whatever…you can tell me. I'm on your side no matter what. You can trust me'.

He nodded. When he spoke his voice sounded hoarse and desperate,

'I think I'm dying.'

'What do you mean? Is there something wrong with you? Have you seen a doctor? What is it?'

The questions tumbled out in a panicky rush. She was confused, scared, and on the verge of bursting into tears herself. Until he explained.

'I had a dream. About me dying.'

'A dream?'

Her voice had swooped up towards a shriek but she managed to suppress it, for fear of waking the children

'A dream?' she hissed, somewhat further down the scale. 'All this…drama …for a *dream*?'

'Let me tell you,' he begged, 'it was so real, Mel.'

And sitting there on the bathroom floor he told her the dream that had been coming to him in fragments over the past few weeks until, finally, last night, it had all come together. In many ways it was a beautiful dream. He talked of a park of endless green; patches of flowers in riots of colours; the sun shining as he enjoyed the day and the company of people he loved all around him. A glow of golden light haloed every plant, every person, even the wooden benches. And, as though he'd been told already, he knew something momentous was about to happen. The knowing was deep inside him. Such a confident feeling. A big change was heading his way. Everyone around was expecting it too. They smiled at him every time he looked toward them, excitement shining in their eyes. Then, a brightly-coloured kite bobbed along toward them, about head height, its string dragging along the grass. As it reached him it paused and he knew... he just knew... that it was *his* kite. Sent specially for him. It hovered patiently beside him, bobbing up and down gently on the softest of breezes. Proudly he grasped the string and the kite rose, carrying him with it, slowly, slowly into the bluest of blue skies while the onlookers smiled and waved. Their love seemed to buoy him up as he drifted away. A feeling of such happiness was in him as he went that tears of joy flowed down his face.

Then he had awoken. Panic had engulfed him. Somehow he felt the dream meant he was going to die. Grabbing hold of Mel, he sobbed again, 'I don't want to die. I don't want to leave you and the girls.' Shocked, Mel held onto him once more, wondering frantically if this was some kind of breakdown from overwork. Or a mid-life crisis. Was forty-two old enough for that? Her mind raced in circles till her practical, mum-will-sort-it-out side reasserted itself. 'It's okay Jamie. This is what we'll do.' And quietly she described how they would let his boss know there was a family emergency and he wouldn't be in today. They'd walk the girls to school together - she figured that a little taste of normality would help a lot - then they would head home and get on the phone. Find a private clinic where he could pay to have a thorough check-up. 'It might take a few days but you'll see,' she finished, 'everything will be all right. There won't be anything wrong.'

Except that.... there was. Something very wrong. 'An aneurism,' the specialist explained after Jamie's CAT scan. Inside his brain. No reason why it was there. Just the possibility that his blood pressure, having soared of late, may have been a factor. Usually for an aneurysm of this size they would be scheduling surgery. But Jamie was unlucky. The position was such that surgery itself would cause irreparable damage. Without surgery Jamie might still have years of life ahead. Or the aneurism could rupture in the next minute.

Afterward they stumbled to the car and Mel drove them home. They were like zombies, as they tried to absorb the shock of the news they had received. Over the next few weeks they started to talk, haltingly, and with many tears, about the risk of Jamie dying suddenly. But one problem seemed insurmountable. What could they say to the girls? Should they wait to see what happened? Or should they try to prepare them and, maybe, alarm them unnecessarily? They had already let their immediate families know and Jamie's boss had been informed. It was he who had arranged for paid leave for a month, to allow them time to come to terms with the situation. The girls were delighted with their daddy's 'holiday' and slowly Jamie began to relax. The dream hadn't returned but he was still convinced it had come as a warning. And then one evening he offered to put the girls to bed on his own while Mel watched a favourite programme. After a while she wandered upstairs to join in with story time. The girls were in their pyjamas, cuddled up to Jamie. Tendrils of damp hair clinging to newly-washed faces. Mia's thumb firmly wedged in her mouth. Listening to the story of Daddy's kite. Standing unnoticed in the doorway Mel listened too. In Jamie's words the story came alive. Of course, there were questions. Where was Daddy going with the kite? When would he be coming back? She listened as he gently answered. As he finished Isabella looked at him solemnly and said, 'But you're not going yet, are you daddy?' He smiled and told her 'no'.

Over the next few weeks the most requested story was 'the one about daddy's kite'. And one weekend Jamie got out his long-abandoned paints and began painting vivid, brightly-coloured scenes from his story. He put the girls into the paintings. And Mel. Everyone looked so happy in them. Finally he bound the paintings together to make a picture book. And slowly life settled down. Jamie had gone back to work but had been moved into a less-demanding job. Lower pay, less stress. As weeks rolled on into months the story became just that – a story.

One warm June day they packed a spur-of-the-moment picnic and went off to the park with the girls. As they ran towards the swings, Mel handed Jamie the bag with the sandwiches. 'I forgot the blanket,' she said, giving him a quick kiss on the cheek. 'I'll just get it out of the boot.' Coming back on her own across the park she noticed people smiling and pointing. There was Jamie in the distance. The girls were with him, shrieking with excitement. Drifting towards them was the most beautiful kite. Golden, gleaming, throwing off light in all directions. She tried to cry out. To stop what might happen. But her throat had seized up tight with fear and dread. As if wading through water Mel found it impossible to move faster, to get to her family. Her legs felt heavy and unbearably slow as she struggled to reach them. There was a dreamlike quality to the place, an unearthly sparkle and joy in the air. Still too far off she saw him reach towards the kite. Across the distance his eyes sought hers and he blew her a kiss before grasping the string in his hand. The kite quivered and began to rise slowly, slowly, into the bluest of blue skies. The girls were waving furiously by the time she reached them and a crowd of people had gathered around, cheering and clapping as he drifted higher. Jamie was laughing down at the three of them. Golden light shimmered around him. Higher and higher he went until all that could be seen was the smallest of golden flashes. Gone.

As if waking from a dream the people around reverted to normal, carrying on blankly as though nothing had happened. Mel held her girls, as they looked to the sky. Beside them Jamie lay on the grass, not moving. The bag had fallen from his grip. He looked asleep, peaceful, absent. Mia tugged at her hand. 'He's not really there mummy,' she whispered. 'I think he's in the story now.'

Rabbit Rabbit

'Will you pick up my other suit from the drycleaners?' Pete asked as he left, briefcase under one arm and slice of toast clutched precariously, along with his jacket, as he elbowed the kitchen door open. 'I need it for that meeting tomorrow. Please?' he added with a little-boy smile in her direction. Lesley sighed to herself as the door closed behind him, and turned back to clearing the breakfast mess away, wondering at the same time how she was going to get the kids to school, head three miles in the opposite direction to the drycleaners which wouldn't be open till eight thirty, and still get to work on time. As the last of the dishes were slammed into the machine she headed to the hall for one more shout up the stairs that she really was leaving *now* and anyone requiring a lift should be downstairs immediately. Some ten minutes later Chloe and Grant were finally gathered. A loud argument ensued about whose turn it was to be in the front seat, at which point Lesley's temper snapped and she yelled at them both to get in the back. They sulked all the way to their drop-off point. Not right outside the school, of course. Apparently it wasn't cool to be seen with a parent. Parents should not be seen - but could be constantly harried.

'Don't forget Melissa and Kara are coming over tonight to work on our history project,' muttered Chloe as she clambered out. 'I don't want another fiasco like last time.'

The fiasco had consisted of Lesley cooking a 'proper' tea of chops, potatoes and veg. The girls had looked horrified.

'We usually have burgers and chips,' Melissa had explained patiently, as if talking to a child.

'No way can I eat that,' chimed in Kara, 'I'm ninety per cent vegetarian.'

The other ten per cent was, apparently, given over to burgers and doner kebabs. Chloe had sat there, crimson in the face, mortified by her mother's lack of understanding. Obviously Lesley's day would now have to factor in some extra shopping. Or could she get away with phoning for a takeaway?

The pre-work queue at the drycleaners meant she was nearly ten minutes after her usual time getting to the office. She worked for a charitable foundation, dealing with grants for all manner of worthy causes and desperate individuals. Knowing how much work was already backed up, and being a scrupulous person, she carried on through the morning without taking a break. With so much to occupy her mind, she was able to ignore the feelings that had dogged her since half past five, when she had jerked awake from a dream. One that had left her in such a state she had been unable to lie in bed any longer and had been forced to leave the warmth of the winter-weight duvet and Pete's unconscious embrace, and tiptoe down to the chilly kitchen for a consoling cup of tea. It was a variation of a dream she had been having repeatedly during the past few months. It made no sense and, being a fairly down-to-earth and practical person, she knew that she should just shrug it off as a bit of a nightmare. Just a dream. But she couldn't. It left her feeling horrified, very tearful, and incredibly guilty. How could she feel guilty over something that hadn't happened? It was stupid. Yet each time she experienced one of these dreams the feelings it evoked stayed with her all day. This time the dream had involved a rabbit. Yes, a rabbit. Lesley had never had a pet rabbit in her life so why she should have one in her thoughts was a mystery to her. For some reason she was showing friends around the house. They went out into the garden where there was a little hutch to one side of the patio. At this point she suddenly remembered that she had a rabbit to look after, but had completely forgotten about it for days or even weeks. Had left it without food, water, care. The rabbit was in an appalling state and either close to dying or actually dead. As soon as she 'remembered' about the animal she was overcome with horror at the plight of the poor little creature. In real life she would never do anything to harm a living creature. She found it impossible to watch a film with pretend cruelty, and as for stories of actual animal cruelty in newspapers or on tv... well, they were heart-breaking. But in this dream she was the cause of the suffering. The guilt and anguish she felt were so strong they had lifted her out of her sleep on a sob. Downstairs, waiting for the kettle, she had found much confusion in her mind. Logic said 'There is no rabbit. Your mind was just playing around with jumbled up ideas while you slept.' But it still *felt* like the rabbit was real.

Sitting sipping tea, she tried to be rational but the feelings persisted. She ended up crying. Perhaps she was depressed? But there was nothing to be depressed about. She had a job she loved. She was overworked, but believed her efforts really made a difference. She and Pete had a rock-solid marriage, even after twenty years, and as for the children, they may have started in on the dreaded teenage years but they were basically good kids. And she and Pete loved them to bits. Worried about them. Were exasperated by them. But always loved them. She knew her family took her for granted and somehow she had fallen into the trap of trying to be a working woman and some sort of super-mum, but that didn't mean she was depressed.

So perhaps this was the start of all the menopausal changes. Lesley knew some women experienced them quite early but was a bit vague about the details. As soon as she got a chance she should see the doctor, get checked out. She had an idea there was some sort of test that could be done.

All this receded into the background as she ploughed her way through application forms and prepared reports and budget statements. By one o'clock she had made some headway and was just thinking about popping to the coffee shop around the corner to pick up a latte and a sandwich when she noticed her mobile phone on the corner of the desk. The message light was flashing. 'Damn!' she muttered, as she read the name of her caller. It was Amy, wondering when she would arrive for their regular every-two-months get-together. She and Joanne were already at the restaurant. 'Sorry!' Lesley called towards the mouthpiece, as she wriggled her arms into her jacket sleeves whilst hanging on to both the phone and grabbing her car keys. 'I completely forgot. But I'm on my way right now. Just order me something with fish, and a glass of white wine, will you?'

Lesley had been friends with Amy and Joanne since schooldays. Somehow, in spite of the different paths their lives were taking, they managed to stay in touch. And their meetings were an important part of Lesley's life. In fact, they were the only part of her life that was just for her. Not her family. Just her. It was usually something she looked forward to. A bit of female gossip. Some sharing of the news in each of their lives. And a chance for Lesley to reconnect with herself too. How had she managed to forget about it?

'Sorry,' she said again as she slipped into the third chair around the table. 'I'm all over the place today.'

Joanne leaned over and patted her hand. 'Don't worry; we're still waiting for the food. And we've saved the best bit of gossip till you could join us.'

She waved her other hand in the air and both of her friends whooped as they spotted the ring on one of her carefully manicured fingers.

'Oh my god, an engagement ring!' shrieked Amy. 'How many does that make?'

'Only three,' Joanne answered, a note of defensiveness in her voice. 'But this time it's The Real Thing. I won't be calling this one off.'

'Right,' grinned Lesley, 'let's have all the gory details.'

Joanne's engagement got them all the way to dessert, as the others bombarded her with questions and demanded to see photos. 'Gorgeous!' was the verdict, both on the new fiancé and the desserts. Though it was fun, underneath the laughter Lesley was still feeling out of sorts and, knowing her as they did, the other two picked up on it. As they waited for their coffees to arrive Lesley was persuaded to share whatever it was that was bothering her. When she recounted her dream she actually had tears coming. It was mortifying.

'I feel so stupid! It was only a dream but it really upset me.'

Amy was already pulling her phone out of her bag.

'Let's get googling,' she suggested.

'Oh, and what are you going to look up?' asked a cynical Joanne. 'My friend dreamed she'd killed a rabbit?'

Amy raised her eyes and sighed.

'You know nothing my dear. The whole world is at my fingertips. There must be someone out there who's had a similar dream.'

She typed in 'dreams'. Followed by 'small animal' and 'neglected, dying'.

'Oh my god!' she exclaimed, seconds later. She looked up at Lesley and in a dramatic voice intoned, 'you...are...not...alone!'

'Seriously,' she continued, 'there's loads of stuff. Apparently this kind of dream isn't at all unusual.' She started to read some of the entries and very quickly some common elements emerged. Firstly, that the animal may represent a part of Lesley's self. A part she was neglecting. And that maybe a creative part of her was being stifled.

'Rubbish!' was the dreamer's verdict. 'My life is about as full as it could get. I've got a wonderful family, a lovely home, and a job I really enjoy. It was just a daft dream and it only upset me because I'm a bit hormonal at the moment.'

She gulped down the last of the coffee.

'Okay, girls, I'm going to have to dash off now. I was in the middle of something at work and I must finish promptly today, we've a busy evening. See you next time!'

She pulled out some cash and left it for the others to sort the bill. And with that, she was gone, waving through the restaurant window as she hurried by.

There was a pause, then,

'Are you thinking what I'm thinking?' asked Joanne.

'Uh-huh,' nodded Amy in full agreement.

At school they had both admired Lesley's talents in art, design, dressmaking. She seemed to create the most wonderful things from very unpromising materials. As a teenager she made most of her own clothes. Designed them and then stitched them together. They were quirky, individual, pieces but so well-made people who didn't know her assumed they were by some expensive designer. Sometimes they'd coax her into making outfits for them too. It was always the plan that she would go on to study design in some way but it hadn't happened. Her parents divorced when she was just finishing A levels and her whole life was in turmoil. She got a job in an office and within a year or two had met Pete.

'Do you think that's why she throws herself into being Perfect Wife and Perfect Mum?' asked Amy. 'I mean, her parents breaking up like that, it was so sudden, maybe she's creating the perfect unbreakable family.'

'Good point. But where's it going to get her? Children leave home eventually. Then it'll be just Pete, the job, keeping the house clean.'

Joanne sighed. 'It's not a life I've ever wanted but I can see the appeal. I just don't think it should have taken her over so completely. I mean, what does she have outside her family and work?'

They thought for a second, then said in unison,

'Nothing.'

'All that talent...' added Joanne. 'Whatever happened to it?'

It was definitely going to have to be takeaway, Lesley decided as she rushed off to pick up Grant. Chloe had insisted on travelling home with Melissa and Kara. Kara's mum would be driving them and she had a car Chloe described as 'supercool'. Apparently Kara's mum was as supercool as her vehicle. She wore expensive designer outfits to some high-powered job in the city. And that job had funded, among so many things, a holiday home in Florida to which they jetted off at every available opportunity. Lesley knew her daughter was desperately hoping for an invite to join them one day.

She'd had trouble concentrating that afternoon. The bits off the internet that Amy read had somehow got to her. At one point she actually looked them up herself. There really was a lot on the net about these dreams, which should have been reassuring. But she was definitely still bothered. It was only when Grant was in the car and she was asking about his day that it all clicked together in her head. He was telling her about his art and design project. He had to come up with a logo or main design for a new t-shirt. Before she knew it, she was telling her son about her design talents, back when she was his age. He didn't seem impressed. It was a case of 'Yeah, mum, whatever..'. She was silent the rest of the way, just remembering and thinking. She had been genuinely talented. Why had she just let it drop? She had no idea. But she did think maybe she could help Grant with his project later. And find out if the old skills were still there.

It all went to the back of her mind when the girls arrived. Lesley had ordered in some Chinese for them but cooked as normal for the rest of the family. Chloe's room was going to be a bit whiffy after they'd eaten up there but that wasn't her problem. Through the ceiling the thump thump of some dirgey music, punctuated by shrieks and giggles, probably meant they weren't getting too much of their work done, but with fourteen-year-olds a mum had to tread carefully.

She hovered around after tea, gently reminding Grant every now and then that he really should get on with his design project. But first he was 'busy' texting friends. Friends he'd spent the day with, so why the need to get in touch so soon? He just shrugged her off. Then he 'needed' to check emails. And Twitter. And then he started to get out one of his video games. That was when she put her foot down and insisted he get on with homework. As if to annoy her, he pulled out maths and then some science work. With much sighing and pen chewing, he plodded his way through the set tasks. By the time he'd finished it was getting on for eight o'clock. What about the design project?

'What's all the fuss about?' he grumbled, turning back to the computer, 'it's no big deal. It'll take five minutes. Tops.'

Sure enough, less than ten minutes later, he pulled a piece of paper off the printer and shoved it carelessly into his project folder.

'There,' he announced, 'that'll do. Now, if you don't mind, I'm going to have some time to myself before the Gestapo order me up to bed.'

He fished out a console, plugged himself in, and hunched over, his thumbs working furiously.

With Grant fully immersed in a world of murder and mayhem, Lesley gently hooked the paper out and looked at it. At first glance it seemed a very neat presentation. He'd created a simple design, printed it off with name, class, project details at the top. Except there was no actual designing involved, just a bit of what she thought of as internet trickery. He'd googled the word 'logo'. Found one he liked. Made a couple of minor adjustments. Then called it his own. She was appalled. Where was the originality in which she had taken so much pride when she was a teenager? Where was the desire to be original? What about the craftsmanship of the work?

The headphones were snatched from Grant's ears, while his mum brandished the piece of paper.

'It's the CND logo!' she accused, horrified.

'All you've done is blank out one small line and turn it upside-down. But anyone would recognise it for what it is. How on earth can you call this a 'design'? Aren't you ashamed of yourself for ripping off someone else's work?'

Her son was genuinely mystified by her concerns. It *was* his design since he'd altered it. In a world where music could be 'sampled', and clothing wasn't copied from the past but was fashionably 'retro', the word 'original' seemed irrelevant. He insisted the rest of his class would have done the same – if they'd even bothered to change things. And that it was more about the ability to manipulate computer images than trying to find a shape or pattern no-one else had come up with.

In the end she gave up trying to convince him. Later, after she'd done her gestapo bit, she showed the paper to Pete. He, too, was unfazed by what she saw as copying. Then, with a gleam of mischief in his eyes, suggested she should have a go at it herself to 'show him how it's done.' With that, he got up to go in the snug and switch on tv. 'Coming? he asked. She shook her head. 'I might give it a go with this,' she told him, brandishing Grant's project – and calling her husband's bluff.

She pulled out a wad of paper and some pencils. Sat looking at the top blank page, trying to let her mind empty and waiting for inspiration. Nothing came. She sharpened the pencils. Straightened the pile of paper. Sat for a bit longer. Still nothing. After twenty minutes of feeling as blank and empty of ideas as the paper, she doodled the original CND logo. Then she doodled her son's version. It looked like a Y in a circle. Now, if he'd put the word 'why' underneath, that would have been a bit more creative. She doodled that version too. Then another that had 'why why why' spaced around the outside of the circle, forming a second ring. She rather liked that one. Just at that moment there was a movement in the corner of her vision. She glanced round. There was nothing there that shouldn't be there, and nothing moving. Then, on her other side, she heard a movement. Just a quiet, padding sound as something went past. If they'd had a cat she would have assumed that's what it was. Her head whipped around. Nothing there. She bent down slowly, afraid of what she might see, and looked under the table. To her relief, the carpet was clear. She sat back up - and came face to face with the largest brown rabbit she had ever seen. It sat not quite square on to her. Its ears at a rakish-looking ten to two. Its velvety nose huffing gently up and down. One large brown eye looking straight at her, while the other seemed fixed on the computer screen. Mesmerised, she slowly reached out a hand and touched its furry head. So soft. She stroked it gently, hardly daring to breathe. From the hallway Pete called out on his way to the kitchen to ask if she'd like a cup of coffee. She turned and hissed at him to come in. He did, smiling slightly quizzically.

'What is it?'

He looked at the table.

'Oh, not bad. You've kind of taken Grants' idea and run with it. I like the why, why, why business. Very cryptic.'

Lesley sat bemused. She'd turned back to see ... no sign of the rabbit. Not so much as a tuft of fur. And she hadn't heard it move. She glanced about.

'You didn't see anything when you walked in, did you?'

Pete shook his head, then his expression cleared with sudden understanding.

'Oh-oh, you've seen a spider somewhere, haven't you?' Where is it?'

It was Lesley's turn to shake her head. 'S'gone now,' she mumbled.

Off he went to the kitchen to make the coffee, muttering about the daftness of anyone scared by a tiny creature like a spider, while she sat there stunned.

She hadn't just seen the rabbit. She'd heard it. She'd touched it. If this was hormonal she was in big trouble. And if it wasn't her hormones playing up, oh hell, she must be losing her mind. Looking back at the paper, and the Y in the circle, she was reminded of the way the rabbit's ears had stood. Ten to two. Idly she redrew the circle but this time added two ears where the arms of the Y had been. Beneath them she drew the rest of the head of the rabbit, one eye slightly to the front. Cute but not enough attitude for a t-shirt design. She frowned. Thought a bit. Then drew it once more. This time she made the rabbit's mouth open in a wide snarl, two vicious top teeth threatening, while above them the half-visible eyes had a mad glint to them. Attitude! She liked the effect. Underneath the circle she wrote the words RABBIT RABBIT, 'just because', as she said when Pete came in with the coffee and asked why.

She decided enough was enough. No more rabbits! A quiet evening snuggling up in front of the tv – even if it was a football match – sounded much healthier. And if she fell asleep leaning on Pete's shoulder, so what?

It was Pete's turn for the school run the next day, which allowed Lesley to work later. She had pushed all the craziness of the last couple of days to the back of her mind. Her day had gone well and she was feeling much calmer when she got home. Where she found an excited Grant waiting to hurl news at her. He'd seen her efforts at creating a logo and had picked them up with his own work. Just to show his teacher. Really. ('Hah!' thought Lesley, 'the little so-and-so probably thought he'd hand it in as his!) But she accepted his explanation and was glad that he hadn't succumbed to temptation. Instead he'd shown his mum's drawings and explained how 'she used to be good at this stuff' when she was young. The teacher had got very excited and passed them round the class. He said it showed a clear progression of ideas which might help them take their own designs to the next level. They'd been given time then to look at each other's work and make suggestions how to develop them. In the end, the class produced some very good quality and original ideas, which they were going to print up on real t-shirts the next week. They were going to have a stall at the next school fair to sell their work, and the person whose work was most popular would win a special prize.

Lesley was thrilled that her own drawings had prompted such enthusiasm. But Grant wasn't finished yet. At the end of the lesson the teacher asked him to thank his mum for letting them look at her work (not that she'd been consulted, but still…) and to tell her that she hadn't lost her touch.

At that she actually got away with hugging her son. He was so excited about the whole episode that he forgot to squirm away. Pete high-fived him, and then he hugged Lesley too. It was a very happy threesome who sat eating their tea and chatting, when Chloe burst in the door from her choir practice.

'Is it true?' she panted. 'Are you making t-shirts? Only a girl in year 10 said she'd seen your design and it was totally wicked. Can I have the first one? And then can you do one for Kara?'

Lesley couldn't remember the last time her daughter had said so much to her all in one go. She glanced at Pete, who shrugged, then at Grant, who grinned.

'I might make a few. Keep them exclusive, you know? But Grant's in line for the first one. I suppose I could put you and Kara next on the list…'

With a whoop, Chloe flung her arms around Lesley's neck and gave a quick squeeze before hurtling upstairs to call her friend.

'Well,' said Lesley, smiling at her son and husband, 'aren't I the popular one!'

'Are you really going to make them, mum?'

She laughed. 'I don't have much choice, do I?'

Pete reached over and put his hand on top of hers.

'You know what, love, it's been too long since you indulged your artistic side. Why don't you take some time to yourself to find out what else you can come up with? If you get a few things together I could set up a website for you. Sell stuff on-line.'

'And I could take some into school,' Grant chipped in, bubbling over with enthusiasm. 'You could set up … ', he furrowed his brow, thinking hard, '…Rabbit Enterprises!'

'Hare Shirts,' added his dad.

'Bunny Business!'

'Window Hopping!'

The pair of them hooted with laughter. She grinned. It wasn't such a bad idea. Chloe thumped back downstairs and threw herself into the empty chair, helping herself from the dishes while the others filled her in on their suggestions. Lesley leaned back in her chair watching her family. And the rabbit. He'd been sitting on the table all through the meal, although no-one else seemed to be aware of him. Once or twice he'd hopped closer to her and she'd stroked him, surreptitiously. He still felt as real and solid as anything around her. He'd filched the odd bit of lettuce from plates, again without the others noticing anything amiss. Now he looked right at her. Slowly, deliberately, he winked one big brown eye. She giggled to herself. Can rabbits wink? Maybe that could be her next design. She'd get drawing straight after tea. It seemed her creativity was well and truly out of the hutch.

Angels

Sally had believed in angels for as long as she could remember. There had been many instances in her life where she just knew that she had been helped or saved by the intervention of a higher force – her angels. Sometimes these were mundane, everyday matters. The way she always got a parking space just as she had asked her 'parking angel' to provide one. Amazing! She would be cruising through a car park saying 'OK, I know you've sorted one out for me. I'm looking for it...' and suddenly a space would open up. Someone would wave to let her know they were just getting into their car and leaving, or maybe a car would just start to nose out of a space as she was reaching it. Or she would be on her way to the office and the traffic would come to a complete standstill. She would send a silent plea to her 'traffic angel' and, sure enough, the cars and lorries would start to thin out and she'd be on her way again. Sally had a variety of angelic helpers – the technology angel (for when her computer or tv went on the blink), her weather angel (for moving rainclouds away), her lost property angel (for when she couldn't find something).... She hadn't decided whether or not there really were all these angels hovering around, waiting to sort things out for her. Maybe just one or two guardian angels that looked after everything between them? Anyway, it didn't matter. If there was a problem she knew how to ask for help.

Sally was convinced that on at least one occasion her life had been saved by an angel. She had been about to cross the road by the traffic lights but, as she stepped into the road, a car came right at her, the driver ignoring the red stop light. She had a split second to realise that she could not get out of the way in time to avoid being hit but sent out an instantaneous thought of 'Help me, please!' As she did so, a man standing behind her at the kerb had lunged forward and grabbed her arm, pulling her back to safety. She felt the brush of the air displaced by the car's speed and knew it had been a very close thing. Of course she had thanked the man, who made sure she was all right before going on his way. Inside though she thanked whoever it was 'up there' who had heard her cry for help and sent him along just in time.

So Sally believed in angels and their willingness to help with problems. It was a bit of an obsession, as she admitted to herself. She filled her world with angels. There was a silver angel on a chain around her neck. An angel screensaver on her computer at work. The house was crammed with angel pictures and ornaments. She had just about every book ever written about angels, some of them signed by the authors. And her all-time favourite film was 'It's A Wonderful Life'.

It wasn't a hobby she felt comfortable writing about to her old friends and there were no new ones to share it with. While her parents had been alive they had shown an indulgent interest in each new acquisition but she had been on her own for some time now. Without Mum and Dad and all the many tasks she had done for them, the hours outside work passed very slowly. It seemed to Sally that she lived in a little bubble, isolated from the rest of the world. She watched other people getting on with their lives but didn't know how to connect with any of them.

At one time she'd led a very different kind of life. An outgoing, popular girl at school, she'd kept in touch with a number of friends after leaving. She had found a secretarial post with a large firm of accountants and had worked her way up to the position of Office Manager. She didn't have any close friends on the staff – they were just colleagues – so for some years her old pals were the mainstay of her social life. She even had an ex-classmate as her fiancé. Not that she'd had much to do with Greg when they were at school. He was studying different subjects from Sally so she only knew him to nod to and say hello in passing. But one of her friends had been in Greg's class for maths and later introduced the two of them. They had dated for about eighteen months before Greg asked her to marry him. The engagement was supposed to be for a year, while they saved for a wedding and honeymoon, and maybe a down payment on a place of their own. But somehow, with Greg living at home and Sally just a few streets away, still with her parents, they had drifted on for nearly three years. Always planning for a future together but both too comfortably settled to make the effort to move things along. Slowly the love they'd had dwindled till one day they both realised they had somehow missed their chance. They agreed to have some time apart to sort out their feelings but within weeks Greg had met someone else. And within three months they were married. Sally had seen him once or twice after that and was able to chat politely and wish him well, though never without a pang of loss. Eventually he and his wife had moved out of the area following a change of job. Some time after, she'd heard from friends that they had a couple of children and seemed to be doing well.

Sally's parents helped her through that particular time. They had always treated her like a little princess – she had been a late and much longed-for child - and now they coddled her more and more. While she was at work being Miss Efficiency, she sometimes thought it was rather ridiculous to be so dependent upon her parents. She often told herself she should get a life. Get out there and do something. Maybe travel. Or find an adventurous hobby. Maybe even another man.

But she continued to live as always. Holidays were spent at the family caravan in Wales. Weekends they might take a picnic out somewhere, or go for a gentle hike. Maybe she would accompany her father to a garden centre to help choose the next season's bedding plants and Saturday mornings were always spent shopping with her mother. Evenings drifted by with them chatting in front of the tv, discussing the latest happenings in their favourite soaps. Occasionally they would get out the cards and play a few hands. The three of them fitted together so well, she could almost believe she didn't need anyone else. She could almost believe they were the same age.

Her friends were all busily getting on with things. Gerry had travelled to the States and ended up marrying a personal trainer and settling in California. The photos she sent showed a very different Gerry from the schoolgirl Sally had known. Whip-thin, tanned, blonde. And after close scrutiny, Sally felt sure there had been some surgical intervention. There were suggestions that Sally might fly over for a holiday but somehow the time never seemed to be right. Meanwhile madcap, adventurous, always-getting-into-trouble Jen had become a Mother. Not just an ordinary mother but one who had made a career out of caring for her huge brood of six. Five girls and a boy. She always said she'd stop once she had a son, and did so... but claimed if Giles had turned out to be another girl she would have happily kept going. Eight children, ten ... She had looked wistful at the thought. Still there were always the grandchildren to look forward to...

They didn't see much of each other now, partly because of Jen's family commitments and partly because they didn't have much in common any more. Sally sighed, thinking how their once-tight group had drifted away. Two other friends had moved to London to work, another was living near Newcastle with her latest man. They all continued to send cards at Christmas and for birthdays, sometimes with a hastily scribbled note inside to up-date her on the events in their lives. She rarely wrote anything inside the cards she sent. There just wasn't any news to pass on.

By the time she had reached her thirties her parents were beginning to rely more and more on Sally. Not that she begrudged the help they needed. They had always been such loving parents to her, it felt like a privilege to give something back. Dad remained pretty spry well into retirement but her mum had succumbed to breast cancer. It had been a long and heart-breaking time, caring for her as she struggled through surgery and chemo. For a few years it looked as though the fight had been won, but then the cancer returned and this time there was no stopping it. After her mum's death the life drained out of her dad. Oh, he tried to keep going and keep cheerful for Sally's sake but they both knew it was a forced cheeriness.

Within a year of becoming a widower, he had the first of a series of heart attacks. Sally nursed him through each one, hovered over him each day with his pills, prepared meals for him to eat while she was out, and then fretted about him all the time she was in the office. It wasn't easy being sole carer. Once upon a time they had known all the neighbours in the street and could have called upon any one of them for help. But now only strangers lived nearby. Mostly young couples with small children. Sally had been vaguely aware of their arrivals over the years but had never got to know any of them. And the only family left was a great-uncle Sally had never met.

When her dad died Sally was truly alone. It was a very strange feeling to be cast adrift in the world so completely. No brothers or sisters. No parents. No husband or children. No friends to speak of. No neighbours to lean on. The funeral had been a very quiet one. Just a couple of people who remembered her father from work, years before, and a few people from the church and the local bowls club. She had asked them back to the house afterwards for a bit of tea. There had been some stilted conversation, some promises to keep in touch, kindly-meant offers of help should she need it. But soon they were gone and the silence in the house folded around her.

Her boss at work had told her to take a bit of time, to try to get over things, before returning but she went straight back. At least she had some company at work. Not that she ever let on about her loneliness. Over the years she had cultivated the idea that she was a person who valued her privacy. Any colleague who tried to get closer was always very politely steered away. So now that she really needed an occasional invitation – perhaps to join a group after work for a drink, or to one of their regular outings – such offers never came her way. Everyone had learned the message that Sally was a self-contained person, with a busy and fulfilled life outside the office, and it was just assumed that she would not want to be involved. For years, pride kept her from letting on that, frankly, she didn't have any kind of a life. She would have hated others to know how dull and restricted it was. Sometimes she might let slip in casual conversation bits of information gleaned from a friend's hasty note, but she would make it sound as though she and her old friends were in fairly constant contact. When she mentioned a play or film that was on she let people think she had been to see it with her friends. Or she might let drop that a certain restaurant in London was a fabulous place to go if you happened to be in the city. A bit pricey but the sea food was exceptional. Everyone assumed she had been there herself, instead of just reading about it in the Sunday supplement. It was the same sense of pride that had stopped her hurling herself at Greg all those years ago when he suggested the 'temporary' split; that had prevented her from howling her refusal at him and begging for another chance to find their way back to love; that then enabled her to smile and chat in a neutral way when she bumped into him with his wife. She clung to it still, though it had never served her well.

At night on her own in an empty house she tried to fill the time with reading and tv. She could spend an hour or two washing and dusting her angel ornaments. Household chores were things to do slowly, savouring the necessity. She never used the dishwasher but washed and dried by hand. She only used the washing machine for heavier items like bedding, preferring to use up more of her time by handwashing her clothes. There would be long cooking and baking sessions after which she would fill the freezer with home-made cakes, lasagnes, fish pies – few of which would ever be eaten. Inevitably most of them ended up in the bin after a frosty six months of hanging around. Sometimes she'd take the car and just drive around the local streets, pretending she had places to go, glancing into lighted windows as she passed and trying not to admit to her loneliness. Weekends, bank holidays and Christmases were so much worse. She tried to stay in bed later in the morning and go to bed earlier at night, just to shorten the days. If the library was open she could while away a few hours there. She would always read the community noticeboard and sometimes wondered about following up on one or two of the activities available, but somehow always held off. After so long on her own she felt paralysed with shyness at the thought of going somewhere new. So when everyone else grumbled about 'being back here again' on their return to work, she joined in. While relief at the return to a busier routine washed over her. And so time rolled on, with Sally getting older and life getting shorter. Halfway through, yet she felt as though she hadn't even started to live.

She chatted to her angels all the time now for want of anyone else to talk to. Sometimes she could imagine that they had answered and would then explain why it was impossible for her to take their advice about getting out, meeting people, joining some organisation. She just couldn't do it. But at the same time she was aware of a growing desperation, a slow slide into depression. She needed help. And that was mostly what she told the angels.

'If you could just find a way to help me meet some nice people... Not at a club or anything like that. I know I wouldn't fit in. Perhaps you could sort out some way for me to chat to some like-minded people....'

Her pleas for help didn't seem to be getting her anywhere. They remained unanswered and for the first time she began to doubt her angels and their ability to solve all problems.

Then came the accident. She was walking past the small parade of shops near her home. She had noticed the window-cleaner from some distance away, swishing his rubber blade over the windows of the flats above the shops, then wiping it on a cloth. He was whistling happily as he worked and she remembered thinking, 'You don't often hear that nowadays, men whistling as they work.' As she got near, and being somewhat superstitious, Sally stepped off the kerb to walk around the ladder rather than underneath it. There was a shout of alarm from behind her. From very close behind her. Then an impact that threw her to the ground, her head catching the edge of the kerb and her arm twisting awkwardly beneath her. There was a vague memory of people gathering around, trying to help her, and the sound of a distant siren. A confusion of voices, movements, sensations, colours, that washed over and around her but made no sense.

She woke to find herself lying in a narrow bed, the covers wrapped so tightly around her that she could barely move. It was dark but there was a light coming from some distance away. Suddenly a face was smiling down at her.

'You're awake at last, we were beginning to think you didn't want to meet us!'

'You're a nurse,' mumbled Sally, somewhat groggily.

'Yes dear, you're in the General. You had a bit of a disagreement with a bike. There's a nasty-looking cut and some swelling on your head, so you may be feeling a bit disorientated. And I'm afraid you broke your arm, but not to worry, it was a clean break and you're all strapped up.'

She reached for a jug of water from a side table and helped Sally sip some water. Her head was pounding and just raising it from the pillow made her feel dizzy and nauseous.

'Back to sleep now,' said the nurse, and straightaway Sally felt her eyes closing as she slid back into a dream-free sleep.

The next time she awoke Sally had the impression it must be early morning. Grey light filled the ward around her. There were half a dozen beds all humped with sleeping figures. Someone was snoring gently, a rich bubbling sound. As she struggled to sit up the same nurse appeared. Seeing Sally's confusion and anxiety she once again explained why she was in the hospital, 'just a slight concussion', and that after a couple of days of observation she would be allowed home.

'We haven't managed to contact your family yet. Is there someone we can phone? You'll need a few things brought in.'

Sally felt her cheeks grow warm as she explained in a whisper that she had no-one, that she lived alone. The nurse pulled a chair across to sit nearer to the bedside and held Sally's hand. Something about her was so encouraging and non-judgmental that Sally found herself telling all sorts of things about her life. When she came to a halt, Nurse Clarence, for that was the name on her tag, looked at her thoughtfully.

'You know, I shouldn't really do this but if you'll trust me with your door key I'll be going off-duty soon. I could call in at your house – it's only a few streets from me – and maybe I could pick up whatever you need. I could phone your office too, let them know you won't be in for a few days.'

'Oh, thank you. That would be so helpful. Are you sure you don't mind, Nurse?'

'Call me Angie,' she smiled warmly, 'And, no, I don't mind in the least. Just don't go telling anyone or you'll get me into bother!'

They made up a list of things to fetch, and Sally explained how the front door always stuck and needed a special technique to open. She gave the office phone number and the name of her boss. By this time she was feeling drowsy again so Angie insisted she close her eyes and try to get a little more sleep 'before the day-shift come on and wake everyone up for their pills'.

When Sally opened her eyes again the ward was busy with staff to-ing and fro-ing, and patients tottering about dragging their drip stands beside them. Mini tv sets over beds were switched on and talking away, seemingly all tuned in to different channels. Then an elderly woman appeared, pushing a tea trolley that looked as if it might run away with her at any moment. She explained she was a volunteer and made Sally a very welcome cup of tea. Then she staggered off, heaving 'the beast' as she called it toward the next bed. Later in the morning a nurse came to check on her and take her blood pressure. She was a bit too busy to talk much, 'not as much time as the night nurses' thought Sally, who was left with a quick smile and a 'chin up.' A little later a doctor whizzed around, trailing some young students behind him. He gave her a cursory once-over before announcing that, unless she showed any adverse effects, she'd be going home the day after tomorrow. He was already moving away as he spoke. By mid-morning Sally felt exhausted and was just leaning back to try to doze again when a young nurse came to her bedside carrying a bag Sally recognised as one she used for shopping.

'A woman was in earlier to bring your things. I expect you'll be glad to get out of that hospital gown, won't you? It's always good to have your own stuff. Is she a friend of yours, or a neighbour? I thought at first she was probably your daughter but she wasn't able to stop, and then I remembered that you were on the list as *Miss* Watkins, so I thought she wouldn't be your daughter, although these days you can never really tell can you? Still, it was good of her to fetch them so quickly......'

Her voice chattered on as she pulled the curtains around the bed and helped her into her own nightie. Sally let the sounds flow around her but made no effort to reply. In truth she didn't feel up to it, just nodded and smiled now and then. For much of the day she continued to sleep, waking when prompted for pills or food or quick checks on how she was feeling. She slept through most of the visiting hours, waking just as people were saying their good-byes, relieved she hadn't been conscious, to be embarrassed by a lack of visitors.

She was feeling much more alert and back to normal by the time Angie came on duty and was able to thank her when she returned the door-key. The fuzziness in her head had gone and she was thinking more clearly.

'I'm sorry if I went on a bit last night,' she said, avoiding looking directly at the nurse's face, 'I don't normally chat away like that about myself.

'Now don't go getting all embarrassed,' said Angie,' We all need somebody to talk to sometimes. Like your neighbour, Emma.'

Sally glanced at her, surprised. It turned out Angie had bumped into Emma as she was leaving Sally's house. Quite literally bumped into her, as Emma had been looking the other way trying to control her lively three-year-old son. Angie had helped carry her shopping into the house while she grabbed hold of Ethan. They'd got chatting and Angie now told Sally what a hard time her young neighbour was having as a single parent.

At the same time Emma was lying in bed unable to sleep for thinking about that nice nurse she'd met who'd told her about Sally, confined to hospital with not a soul in the world to care about her. 'It's terrible,' she thought, 'eight months I've been here and I've never made an effort to go round and say hello. That poor woman.' She made up her mind to do something about it, then managed to drop off to sleep.

By now Angie was telling Sally about the phone call she'd made to the office.

'Your boss is such a nice man, isn't he? And he relies on you for everything. I think the poor man's going to be lost without you. Apparently all the staff in the office were adrift without you there today. They say you're always in early, never miss a day.'

Sally smiled, grateful that she mattered in some way.

'It's a shame about Tia though, isn't it?'

Sally frowned. Tia was one of the younger girls. She only worked part-time but was forever rushing in late and her mind never seemed to be on her work. But she wasn't aware of any problem. Apparently Angie had no qualms about chatting to complete strangers on the phone and drawing all sorts of information out of them. It was amazing how much she knew. All about Tia's mother moving in with her and the fact that she had multiple sclerosis, needing a lot of help. That was why Tia had accepted a part-time job. Now Tia might have to give up her job altogether as she just wasn't coping too well.

'Oh, I know all about the problems of being a carer,' exclaimed Sally. 'The poor girl, no wonder her work's a bit off.'

Angie smiled to herself remembering how the 'phone call to the office' had in fact been a personal visit. She'd chatted to everyone while she was there, explaining about Sally's accident and that her friends all lived too far away to be able to help out. She'd spent a long time with Tia, saying how much Sally sympathised with her, having cared for both her own parents.

'She did all that,' said Tia, 'And while working here full-time. Wow. It makes me feel a bit useless.'

'Don't talk yourself down' said Angie, 'I'm sure you're doing a great job for your mum. You know, Sally has probably got a lot of expertise you could tap into and I bet she'd love to help. She's just a bit shy about interfering...'

One look at Sally's boss convinced her that here was an interesting situation. Paul was on his own too, and although he had a wide circle of friends and enjoyed playing tennis and going to the theatre, he could probably do with a bit of feminine influence in his life. Home life was not much fun and he tended to live in the most outrageous mess, which was one of the reasons he liked to come to work. The office, by comparison, was a haven of organisation and quiet efficiency. Clearly he had a great admiration for his Office Manager and the way she ran his life so smoothly, so a little suggestion that maybe Sally wasn't finding her job quite as fulfilling as she once had was more than enough to worry him and get him thinking.

As Sally snuggled back into the pillow, yawning once again, Angie's parting shot was to suggest that Paul was quite a lonely man. Too much focus on work, that was his trouble. Maybe once in a while Sally could persuade him to join in with a group of staff, heading out for a Friday night drink or a meal? After all the Office Manager had to be able to manage more than just the obvious stuff. Managing people was a great skill to develop, too.

Sally was very thoughtful the next morning as she took in everything Nurse Clarence had said. She was stunned to realise that she wasn't the only one struggling. That while she shut herself away from fear that people would realise how pathetic her life had become, she also shut herself away from helping people who needed it. Her thoughts were interrupted as the first of the day's visitors began trickling in to the ward. She leaned back and closed her eyes, hoping people would assume she was still tired, but then heard a voice saying her name. There was a young girl there by her bed, clutching a bunch of rather bedraggled chrysanthemums, and Sally recognised her as the neighbour she'd glimpsed going in and out of the house next door. A wriggling imp of a child was struggling to get out of her grip and across the room to something he'd spotted. Sally reached for the button to raise the head of the bed and enable her to sit up, and instantly engaged his attention. Before she knew it he was perched on her bed next to her as she gave him a ride, down then back up, while a grateful Emma fetched a chair and sat down beside her. With a smile she proffered the flowers explaining that they had looked a lot better but then Ethan had insisted on carrying them in the lift and had managed to catch them in the doors when they stopped at a lower floor.

'Never mind,' Sally laughed, 'the thought was there.'

She felt quite overcome that her young neighbour had made the effort to come in and see if she was all right. Ethan had now moved on to examining the items on the bedside table, among them a little angel ornament. She hadn't even realised Angie had put that in the bag. She handed it to him to play with and he seemed content to sit and make it fly through the air (with aeroplane noises) while she and Emma got to know a bit about each other. Suddenly their chat was interrupted as a crowd stopped around the bed. Paul and Tia and a couple of others from the office had arrived with another bunch of flowers – in somewhat better condition than the poor old chrysanthemums – and a large teddy with a sash bearing the legend 'Get Well Soon' across its furry chest.

'It's an angel bear!' explained Tia, pointing out that the bear had padded wings on its back and a halo hovering over its ears. 'We know you like your angels.'

Sally was totally taken aback by their arrival. They had to borrow chairs from a couple of other bedsides and Paul joked that they'd probably get thrown out if the nurses realised she had more than the standard two visitors. She introduced them to Emma, grateful that she hadn't been alone when they arrived, and then found herself the centre of attention as she explained about the accident.

'So let me get this straight,' said Paul, 'in order to avoid the possible effects of bad luck from walking under a ladder, you stepped into the path of a speeding cyclist and got yourself put in the hospital.'

Said like that it did seem a bit funny and Sally had to giggle her agreement. Paul noticed how pink she went in the face and how her eyes crinkled up when she laughed. She looked softer somehow, and less in control. In fact, sitting in the hospital bed, her arm strapped up and a huge plaster on her temple, she looked quite vulnerable. There was a little shift deep inside him as he realised how fond he'd grown of Sally over the years.

It was a lovely visit and Sally enjoyed telling Angie all about it that night when she came on duty. There was a slight self-consciousness in her voice whenever she mentioned Paul, which the nurse smugly put down in her mind as 'very promising'. All in all she felt she'd done a good job. She wished Sally well for the next day, when she would be going home. Emma was going to be there to help her inside and arrangements had been made so that when she returned to the office she'd be able to cope one-handed.

And so it was that a very different Sally left the hospital. Sitting in the ambulance she reflected that if a bang on the head was what had been needed, then it was a good thing she'd avoided that ladder. She sent a fleeting 'thank you' skywards but then caught herself. She wasn't going to give up on her angels but maybe it was about time she started believing in people, too.

Hovering invisibly above, 'Nurse Clarence' watched with satisfaction as the ambulance arrived outside the house. Emma was there, true to her word, and Ethan bounced around them as they made their way in. Yes, all in all, a very good job.

Calendar Girl

The day Michael got the post at Hartwood Primary he thought he'd landed his dream job. The interview process had been quite long and arduous but he had such a passion for what he hoped to do for the school that he'd been able to keep up a high level of energy all the way through. Having researched data on the school thoroughly, he used his two visits there to talk to as many people as possible, getting their views on how the school was doing and where they would like it to head next. He hadn't needed notes for his presentation to the interview panel – he spoke from his heart and from previous experience. The extra studying and preparation for headship that he'd already completed stood him in good stead for many of the questions and written challenges he'd faced. Best of all, his time working as deputy to Sarah at his last school was a tremendous help. She had been that rarity among bosses. Willing to share the power her position gave her and generous enough to share her thoughts and plans. A person who wanted full consultation with others and was prepared to take on board their advice, yet knowing her own mind and willing to step up and take full responsibility when the occasion warranted it. She had been an inspiration and had provided a fantastic boost both to his ambitions for the future and his ability to achieve them.

As soon as he heard that the job was his, he phoned his parents to let them know. They were delighted for him. Hartwood wasn't too far from where they still lived and Michael had grown up. In fact the woodlands for which the school was named had been a favourite picnic and camping place when Michael and his sister were small, although housing now encroached on it. It was an area close to town yet with a semi-rural, 'village', feel. The school reflected this. Most of the children on roll were at least the second generation of their family to attend and it was quite small, just under 180 children ranging in age from three to eleven years. The pupils usually went on to the same high school which meant that many local people had known each other throughout their schooldays and on into adult life.

The present headteacher had been there for over twenty years and was such a fixture in people's lives that Michael suspected they might have trouble adjusting to an incomer when she retired in just three months' time. Still, change had to happen and he would try to be sensitive as everyone got used to a different person in charge. At only thirty-two he would seem relatively young and inexperienced compared to the eccentric, slightly-feared, but much-loved Mrs Tibworth. He suspected the local authority would be quite pleased to celebrate Daphne Tibworth's retirement. She had been a wonderfully charismatic head but many of the changes in education had passed her by during the latter part of her career. Various people had been sent into the school to 'help move things on' only to find themselves 'moved on' by Daphne. Out of the school and back to where they came from. The last Ofsted visit had not rated the school very highly because of discrepancies between their expectations of how a school should be run and Daphne's implacable determination to emulate her favourite singer and do it her way. Over the years results in exams had gradually fallen off and the school didn't seem to be holding up academically against its counterparts. Newcomers to the area took one look at the statistics available via the Internet and decided to take their children further afield for their schooling.

And yet she had built up so much that was good within the school. It was genuinely a part of its neighbourhood, joining in or initiating events throughout the year and forming a hub for social activities in the area. There was a lovely feeling of comradeship among the pupils, older children taking great care of the younger ones, and the staff had formed good relationships with the children in their classes and with each other. The staffroom demonstrated their friendly attitude. It felt like a warm and relaxing haven. He could see himself sitting down in there at the end of a busy day, leading staff meetings or chatting informally about their day and any problems they had encountered, before taking himself back to his office to work and leaving them to enjoy the privacy of their room.

The three months leading up to Christmas and the New Year brought a mixture of emotions for Michael. He was sad that this would be his last term in his current school. He got on so well with everyone and they were all incredibly supportive. Children persisted in coming up to him and demanding to know why he was leaving.

'Oh go on, sir, tell them you can't come and we'll keep you here.'

It was going to be a wrench to say goodbye to all of them. At the same time he was so excited about his new job that he had been making numerous plans. He had also attended meetings with a nearby head who was going to mentor him through the first year. And there had been a very tricky couple of sessions with Daphne Tibworth. She had expounded at length about how she ran the school. And, by implication, how she expected Michael to do it. But he did get time to meet the children at an assembly and then some of the parents afterwards. He had a few quick chats with staff and governors but only at a social level. He didn't want to tread on Daphne's toes. The whole term he felt as though he were at the start of a race, hopping from one foot to the other, pumped up with adrenaline and ready to run but having to wait for the starter's pistol.

He spent Christmas with his parents. Michael's sister Jo came to stay too with her husband Phil and their new baby. He'd done his usual last-minute shopping and produced plenty of appropriate but unimaginative gifts. They on the other hand had obviously got together and themed his presents. There was a beautiful leather briefcase and a very expensive pen from his parents. Jo and Phil had made up a box of individually-wrapped surprises that turned out to be everything they thought he would need for his office. A desk set, a wooden drawer-organiser with compartments for items such as paperclips and rubber bands, an executive toy, a framed photo of the family, even a calendar called 'Office Girl' to hang on his wall. So with good luck wishes ringing in his ears from ex-colleagues, friends and family, he got to January and the start of his new life.

He wanted to be the first to arrive in school so two days before the start of term he let himself in at seven in the morning. The office that was to be his new operations centre was full of Daphne and her time in the school. He wanted to change things around without any staff there to avoid any more upset than necessary. The desk which, for twenty-four years had been firmly planted across the middle of the room, with Mrs T. equally firmly planted behind it, was moved to the wall so he could work but turn away from the desk when visitors came in. He didn't want that huge slab acting as a barrier. He made a pleasant group of furniture in the space that was now available. Three comfortable chairs he had previously earmarked for the purpose around a low coffee table. He set a plant he'd brought with him in the centre of the table. There was a bookcase to one side. He ruthlessly weeded out most of its contents: a syllabus for teaching from the seventies; various documents that had been superseded many times since their publication; books that were falling to bits and had lost part of their contents. He wondered how often Daphne had actually used any book from here.

Then he set up his desk with the items from his family – apart from the executive toy, which he put into a bottom drawer in case anyone thought him frivolous. Finally he turned his new calendar to January and hung it at eye level. Leaning back in the chair he studied the picture. There was a man sitting at a desk – much as he was – and a smiling young woman was fetching him a steaming cup of tea, biscuits on the side of the saucer. The caption read 'Time to get on with some work'. He grinned as he compared the cheery office girl with Deborah Stevens, the school secretary and also his personal secretary. In this small school there wasn't the budget to employ much office support and Mrs Stevens was apparently all that was on offer.

She had provided the only 'off' note he had encountered on his visits. Thin to the point of being gaunt, the lines on her face were more indicative of misery than joy. She had almost scowled at him when he arrived. No cheery greetings had issued from her, no welcome to the school. In fact she was barely civil. His attempts to start a dialogue had been met with brief, sharp replies after which she had returned to her tasks and ignored him. Hmmm. Maybe she was finding the changeover especially difficult. He had tried to ask Daphne about the secretary but had received a blank look and then the explanation that she didn't concern herself with that sort of matter. In other words, since she arrived at the school Deborah Stevens had been allowed to run things however she chose as long as it didn't affect Daphne. He added Deborah to the list of urgent tasks he was keeping in his head.

He could hear the caretaker coming in, grunting with surprise at the opened door, although he must have seen the car parked outside. Michael called a greeting and, a moment later, a head appeared around the edge of the door. The eyes swivelled quickly round, taking in the changes.

'I see you've got settled then.' There was a hint of challenge in the assertion.

Yes, thank you,' Michael replied cheerily but firmly. 'It needed to be done so I could start organising myself. Perhaps you could give me a hand later moving some of these filing cabinets.'

He indicated the three tall cupboards parading down the side wall and they agreed a time for Alan to bring the sack-barrow round and help shift them. After he withdrew his head and closed the door behind him, Michael looked at the cabinets and heaved a sigh. Not a job he was looking forward to. He preferred people to paper but knew he had a lot of sorting and organising to do first. The only filing ever done on Daphne's watch appeared to consist of stuffing papers into drawers and closing them. No file dividers, no labels, no method. He imagined that she must have started with just one cabinet. Then, when that was full, added another, and then another. For all he knew the fourth cabinet might be on order right now. He pulled from his briefcase the roll of heavy duty bin-liners he'd brought with him and got to work. When Alan returned at midday there were several full bags to be removed plus two empty filing cabinets. The remaining one was fitted out with labelled file hangers but very little paperwork. There hadn't been much worth saving.

Michael imagined the records on children, personnel, the budget, and so on, must be kept in the school office and wandered off to look. By now staff were beginning to arrive, setting up their classrooms and enjoying some catch-up chats before the term started properly and they were required to be there. It was therefore quite informal. People were dressed as was he in casual clothes, jeans and jumpers mostly. He stopped to chat with people and wished them a belated Happy New Year. He produced the gift he'd brought for them, a huge tin of biscuits for the staffroom, and stopped to have a mug of coffee with the few who were around. Then he heaved himself to his feet and announced that he had to get in to the office next, he wanted to check out where the records were kept and he needed to move some to his office. There was a brief moment as one or two glanced at him and seemed to be about to say something, then shrugged and moved on. As he left the room he heard one say 'Good luck with that,' in a low voice.

There was a faint noise as he opened the office door so he had time to plaster a smile on his face when he encountered Mrs Stevens.

'Good morning, Deborah,' he said.

She gave a grudging reply without turning in his direction. He stood for a moment and wondered whether he should say a few words about the level of professional respect that should exist between colleagues. It seemed a little heavy-handed though. And they hadn't even started yet. So he gritted his teeth and continued in as pleasant a manner as he could. He told her exactly which documents he required in his office to be able to do his job efficiently. At first there was no reply but as she turned around to face him he saw two spots of high colour had appeared on her cheeks and a red flush of anger was creeping up her neckline.

'That sort of thing is kept in here,' she replied coldly.

'Well, it was for Mrs Tibworth. However, I have a lot to do on writing new school documents, working out assessments, and preparing for the Spring budget. I'm going to need all that information on hand. And you could certainly do with a bit more space in here.'

As he looked around the cluttered office there was no reply but he could feel the heat of anger coming from her.

'Is there a reason why you need them in here?' he asked politely.

No reply.

'I'm sure you have all sorts of pupil and staff records on computer anyway.'

No reply.

'Well in that case I'll just get on and find what I need.'

And that was when Deborah Stevens declared war on him. Not out loud of course, but every single action, every word that issued from her from after that made it absolutely clear she wanted him out of the school.

Within the next few weeks Michael became acutely aware of how easily one person could change things. And not for the better. After an initial welcome the staff had seemed to withdraw from him and it was only after hearing a chance remark that he began to realise the cause. Or at least one of them. Sita, the year four teacher, made an oblique comment about how easy it had been to have a quick word with Mrs T. and nip any problems in the bud. Sensing there was more behind this, he replied that of course his door was always open to staff – unless he was caught up in something he couldn't leave, like a meeting with an adviser or a parent.

'But I've been to see you twice, got an appointment, spent all of my break waiting, and then been told you couldn't see me after all.'

'An *appointment*...? Who said you had to have an *appointment*....'

He caught himself. Stopped. Gave a smile and said,

'How about popping in after school today for a little catch-up? I'm sure you've dealt with the issues by now, but I'd like to talk things through.'

At the next break-time, he hovered in the corridor near the back door to the office - the one that connected down a short passageway to his room - and, sure enough, two members of staff stopped by the front office to ask if there was any chance of having a quick word with Michael. As he listened, Deborah informed them that he didn't want to be disturbed but she would make an appointment for them during lunchtime. 'When she knows perfectly well I have a meeting at County Hall', thought Michael. He pushed open the door, breezed in as though unaware and said 'hi' to everyone.

'Is there a problem?'

'No,' one of them glanced briefly at the secretary, 'we were just making an appointment to see you.'

'An appointment? You don't need one of those! Just come through, and we'll have a chat now.' He turned to the secretary. She wasn't looking too pleased.

'Oh, Mrs Stevens, would you bring through a couple of mugs of coffee? It's bad enough these two will be missing a quiet sit-down, I don't want them to miss their caffeine-fix too.'

As the two went past him through the doorway he turned, and in a voice pitched to ensure the teachers heard clearly, said,

'And you won't forget I'm out at lunchtime, will you? It's in the diary.'

And with a generous smile he swept the two bewildered members of staff through to his office.

He hoped that would put an end to her nonsense. It was bound to get around the staffroom that it was Deborah Stevens blocking them from seeing him. Just to make sure, he put a notice on the staffroom board informing any member of staff wishing to see him did not need to make an appointment but should come straight through and knock. 'If there's no answer it means I'm too busy, and please come back later.' Then as a more-permanent solution he ordered a door system for Alan to fit that would light up a 'PLEASE WAIT' or 'BUSY' or 'COME IN' sign outside his door.

When Sita called in for her after-school chat, she asked if the notice on the board applied to the children too. It turned out several members of staff had been sending children to show best work to Michael but had also been turned away. This made him very angry – the thought of Deborah Stevens disappointing children just to have a go at him was not on. So at the next assembly he announced a regular time each day for children who had done excellent work to come along and show it to him. He blocked the bit of time into his diary and informed Mrs Stevens that he would not be available for other things at that time.

And so it went on like an interminable game of cat and mouse, though who was cat and who was mouse would have been hard to say. Every time he found out about another one of her annoyances he would either tackle it head on or find a way to circumvent her. Gradually he realised how subtle and unanswerable some of her tricks could be. It wasn't easy to actually prove that she was responsible for many of them. Confidential letters from County came in large self-seal envelopes, marked CONFIDENTIAL and addressed to the headteacher, but he soon noticed that these had been opened and resealed. When he challenged her about it, she shrugged, and muttered that it had obviously happened before they'd reached the school. His car keys went missing from a hook in his office so one night he was stuck there for hours searching for them, then had to leave his car at the school and get a taxi home. When he arrived the next morning with his spare keys he discovered the original set lying on his desk with a note from the early-morning cleaner to say she'd found them under his desk. Except of course he'd looked under there. Crawled all around the floor, in fact, checking for his keys. He was as certain as he could be that he knew who was responsible. He just couldn't prove it. Similarly, he'd heard rumours were going around among parents that he wasn't very approachable. Tended to lose his temper. There was a marked drop-off in the number of parents writing or phoning in for a meeting with him. He felt sure this was another bit of nastiness emanating from the office so did his best to counter it by making sure he was outside in the playground before school, on as many days as he could manage, chatting to parents, smiling, offering longer times to talk over any matter that was mentioned to him. Once or twice parents came to see him with a complaint which he dealt with in his usual calm and agreeable way. Then, as they were leaving, they said something to the effect that 'I didn't expect you to be like this.' No, he didn't suppose they had, after Deborah Stevens had spread her poison. And yet again the frustrating thing was - he just couldn't prove she'd done anything.

Towards the end of term he was working on the budget to be presented to the Governing Body. It was very important that he get this right but it was the first time he'd ever had to work out a school budget single-handed. Jobs depended upon him getting this right and the children's progress depended upon his ability to use the available money to best effect. He'd asked Deborah for various printouts of costings and used these as the basis for his calculations. He worked late into the night many times over those weeks. Then came the Budget Meeting. His first big challenge since he'd started his headship. It had to be right. Deborah Stevens was there too, as a staff governor. Apparently none of the support staff had asked to stand as a governor when they knew she wanted the position. A whiff of intimidation hung in the air but there had been nothing Michael could do if other people wouldn't put themselves forward.

He cleared his throat and began to present the budget. Disconcertingly, Deborah Stevens was sifting through a sheaf of papers as he spoke, ticking things off, or looking puzzled or disdainful in turns. The rustling and fidgeting was getting to him and, once or twice, he lost the flow of his words. Then she interrupted him. Loudly.

'That can't be right! The figures from last year are a long way off that.'

He checked again. No, he'd got it absolutely spot on. After all, last year it had been....

'No it wasn't,' she declared.' I've got last year's figures here! It was nothing like that amount.'

The other governors were beginning to look distinctly underwhelmed. His smooth, confident delivery had turned into a shambles. Somehow he had to regain the control and momentum.

'I think it be would best if I continue explaining the budget I've prepared. Then afterwards Mrs Stevens and I can go and check this particular figure against the printouts in my office. This one item won't materially affect any other aspect so, if you agree in principle, I'm sure we can arrange for your Chair to sign off on the budget when this little matter is resolved.'

He managed to pull himself together till the end of the meeting but it was clear that everyone present thought he'd made an error and just didn't want to admit it. His secretary maintained a blank expression but by now he could read her well enough to feel waves of smugness rolling away from her.

Together they went back to his room where he pulled open a drawer in the filing cabinet and removed a file marked 'BUDGET PREP'. He pulled out the relevant printout and, sure enough, Deborah was right. He had transcribed the figure incorrectly, putting the whole thing several thousands of pounds out. He apologised, thanked her for pointing out the error. After she'd left, he slumped in his chair at the desk, paper still in hand. He continued to stare at the paper, at first unbelieving. Then, gradually, rage took over. It wasn't the printout he'd used. It wasn't the printout she'd given him. There were no pencil notes on the paper and he knew there should be. Shaking with fury he marched into the general office but she was long gone. What to do though? If he made a fuss about it the Chair of Governors would assume he just couldn't admit he'd made a mistake. And if he said anything about Deborah Stevens and what she'd been up to they'd think he was losing it big time.

Back in his office he sat thinking for a long while but could come up with nothing except to go along with it. Accept responsibility. Let them think he couldn't be trusted to work out a budget on his own. Sighing, he leaned back and gazed at his calendar. For March there was a picture of the man in the office sitting in a comfy chair, feet up, mug of tea in hand. Outside the door the office girl was smiling brightly at a visitor as she announced that 'Poor Mr Prendergast is *sooo* busy today. Could I deal with it, instead?'

'Oh, yes please!' thought Michael despairingly. 'Oh, to have a secretary like that.'

She smiled so sweetly out from the calendar. Always pleasant. Always looking out for her Mr Prendergast. The caption this month read 'Hard work never hurt anyone.' He smiled back weakly, then dragged himself up from the chair and went home.

He came in extra early the next morning, ready to re-write the faulty section of Budget and to do a covering letter of apology to go with it. He heard others arriving later on, and then the office door. She was here. When the quiet knock on his door startled him, he called 'Come in', and then returned his eyes to his work. A slim hand reached around him with a steaming cup of tea. A soft voice close to his ear said, 'Cream biscuits today, by way of apology. I'm so sorry about that printout. I don't know how I managed to mix up the numbers like that. Still, I've emailed the governors to explain how I got it wrong.' He looked up, bewildered, in time to see a shapely and very short-skirted rear disappear through the door. For a few moments more he sat gaping then pulled himself together and followed a trail of perfume out of the door and into the office. The smiling girl from the calendar was standing there, answering the phone with one hand, using the other to sign for a package from the postman. Perhaps Mrs Stevens was ill and had arranged a stand-in? The postman was clearly smitten, gazing at her adoringly. He stage-whispered, 'Thanks Debbie,' as she finished signing. 'See you tomorrow.' She blew him a kiss, finished the call and put down the phone. Debbie? Where was Deborah? How did the postman know this woman?

Then Sita passed the opened enquiry window as she came into school.

'Hi Sita.'

'Hi Debbie. Catch up with you later!'

The door next to the window opened and the year six teacher, Sandra Dalloway, leaned her head in.

'Good morning, Debbie. Did you manage to get that book order off yesterday?'

'Sure.' Debbie smiled. 'It should be here in three or four days.'

'Fantastic, you're a treasure!'

The door closed and 'Debbie' turned to face him.

'Was there anything else, Mr Stewart?'

Confused to the point of assuming he was either mad or still asleep, he shook his head.

'I'll bring your post through in a moment,' she said. He mumbled a thank-you and stumbled back to his office, half-collapsing into the chair. His gaze drifted up to the calendar. The smiling girl, Debbie, was no longer there. Instead he saw a scrawny, middle-aged woman, her hands on her hips and her mouth wide open. Clearly drawn in mid-harangue. He leaned closer. She bore a startling resemblance to Deborah Stevens. He jerked back in horror. Good God, it *was* Deborah Stevens. And, boy, was she mad at somebody. Then he noticed the caption below. He could have sworn it said something else yesterday. Now the legend read 'Somebody's in for it.'

The rest of the day passed in a sort of dream. Michael found it hard to make any kind of coherent response to anything. His mind was clearly elsewhere. The staff, who were beginning to feel more comfortable with him, noticed he wasn't quite himself and one or two stopped by to ask Debbie if he was all right. Her big blue eyes reflected concern as she told each one she thought he'd been working much too hard lately, what with the budget and everything. They treated him very gently as a result, keeping minor worries away from him and sorting them out between them. And so he had the quietest, most enjoyable day he'd known since starting at Hartwood. He had time to wander round the school, joining in with lessons, sitting chatting to children and staff. Debbie took care of everything, organising him so well he found the day just flowed. And it was so good to be treated decently, to be on the receiving end of smiles instead of glares and frowns. By the time the children left to go home he was feeling quite relaxed. Only then did he realise how much tension he had carried all term, how much negativity he'd been fighting off. Before putting on her coat to go, Debbie popped in and made him promise to go home early for a change. He agreed he would and thanked her, in a most heartfelt way, for her work and support that day.

'You've been wonderful. The perfect secretary.'

She beamed at him. 'But Mr Stewart, you're so easy to work for. I've never had such a kind boss!' And off she went.

His gaze drifted to the calendar and his smile faded. The picture had changed again. The drawing of Mrs Stevens was slumped in a chair, glaring at him. He found himself talking to it as though it were real.

'No-one missed you, you know. Eight years working here, and no-one's even noticed you've gone. I wonder what that says about you?'

He gathered up some papers and put them into his briefcase, then locked up and left.

When he woke the next morning he was convinced it had all been some kind of weird dream. People can't just disappear with no-one noticing. And drawings can't step down from the wall and be real. But he was hopeful enough to stop en route to school and buy some flowers for the office.

Shortly after he'd got stuck into some paperwork his door burst open and a very happy Debbie bounced in to thank him for the lovely flowers. He smiled back, told her it was just a little token for all her work, and she disappeared again to fetch him a cup of tea.

'Definitely chocolate biscuits this morning!' she sang out, as she left.

He laughed and turned back, his eyes once again drawn to the calendar. Mr Prendergast was back. He was standing behind his desk, red-faced with anger, pointing a finger at a very subdued looking Deborah. The caption said 'Staff Training'.

That summer term a quiet revolution occurred at Hartwood. Michael found himself discussing all his plans with Debbie before he even mentioned them to staff or governors, She had a wonderful way of helping him adapt his plans so that they would be more acceptable, of finding ways to broach them so that people were supportive. Exciting developments in the curriculum began to get underway and the teachers seemed rejuvenated by them. The place began to buzz with enterprise and initiative. The school was so well-organised by Michael and Debbie that days ran more smoothly, and staff found their jobs less stressful. The work the children was producing was clearly of a higher standard by the summer break and plans to make even more progress the next year were pretty much finalised. Word had got out that Hartwood was the place to be. A sense of optimism and 'can-do' suffused the place. It was turning into the kind of school Michael had always known it could be, combining the best of past practice with the best of the new ideas. And all because of one person going.

Michael had tried to analyse just what had gone wrong between him and Mrs Stevens. He knew there had been a rather bitter divorce from a Mr Stevens shortly before she had come to work at the school. He knew she had once been at University but had dropped out after a year – maybe to get married? He wondered if she felt dissatisfied with what she had achieved in life. Maybe she thought that, if circumstances had been different, she could have been the one running the school. And in a way she had been until Michael's arrival. She was able to keep all the information and day-to-day organisation to herself. Mrs Tibworth hadn't interfered. Staff had quickly learned that if they wanted stock to arrive on time or access to the head they'd better keep in with Deborah. She had the power to make their lives very difficult if she chose. But of course, she wasn't the head. She wasn't trained in what to do to maximise the children's potential. And she shouldn't have been the one making vital decisions that affected the teaching provision.

When Michael had arrived he had naturally assumed those things were for him to decide, along with the teachers, and had inadvertently taken the power away from her. No wonder she was so angry with him. She thought she knew so much more than some new upstart about running the place. Except that, now Michael and the teaching staff were back in control, everything was improving.

Sometimes before leaving the office he would talk to the image of Deborah in the calendar, explaining what they were now doing and why it worked so much better. He could see by her expression she didn't agree but she was a captive audience. He was always interested in seeing what she was up to and how the caption recorded different thoughts. For some weeks there had been anger but that subsided into sullen indifference. Mostly she just slumped about the place. The glares and threats had gone. Now she just looked at him apathetically. She was, if anything, even thinner than when he had known her. The lines on her face more pronounced. Her skin grey and lifeless. She didn't appear to be taking very good care of herself. Her hair was a mess and needed a trim. And although the outfits she wore changed on a regular basis they were often wrinkled or grubby looking. When Mr Prendergast was in the picture he would invariably be having a go at her about something, making her re-do work, threatening her with losing her job. She didn't look a scary prospect any more.

End of term arrived in a triumph of exam results, Sports Day, social events. The staff stayed around for the first week to sort out room changes, displays, and so on. Then they too went off for a well-deserved break. Michael flew off to Italy for a couple of weeks with friends and returned, brown-skinned and refreshed. He popped in and out of school during the rest of the holidays, doing a few hours' work each time. Occasionally meeting up with staff doing the same. Then there was a flurry of activity during the last week, including a couple of staff training days. Before he knew it Michael was starting his third term as Head and looking forward to the year immensely.

Finding himself back at his desk at eight o'clock on the first official day, he realised his calendar was still showing July, with Deborah Stevens slumped despairingly at her desk. He turned the page over. August. And Deborah wasn't just slumped, she was sobbing, hands over her face, tears trickling through her fingers. The caption read 'Work is such fun!'

Michael felt a twinge of pity. She looked dreadful. He had just turned to September but, before he had a chance to see the new picture, Debbie knocked. She walked in slowly, carefully balancing a mug and a pile of letters.

'Isn't it lovely to be back!' she beamed at him.

'Yes,' he laughed. 'We're in for a lot of work this year but, yes, it *is* good to be back.'

They discussed the diary for the week, with Debbie making one or two of her usual sensible suggestions, then off she went to answer the phone. Looking down at the calendar he was still holding, he saw the September picture. The pathetic figure that had been Deborah was slumped on the floor. The starkly-worded caption below just said, 'I'm sorry.'

For the first time he felt truly sad for her. She had made mistakes but perhaps he could have handled things differently, won her round in time. It was such a waste that she had ended up like this. 'And for what?' he asked the picture quietly, 'Just a bit of nastiness. I don't suppose you were always like that. Maybe if you'd made one or two different choices, you could have been like Debbie. She's so popular, everyone loves her. And she really makes a contribution to the school. We couldn't achieve as much if we didn't have her, running the office so well, helping me do the best job I can.' He shook his head, sighed, and placed the calendar in the drawer where he wouldn't have to see what became of her next.

Carrying an empty mug he walked through to the office with a list of letters that needed replies sent. As he walked Debbie turned and said 'Hello,' in a quiet voice. Except it wasn't Debbie. His lovely, smiling, happy Debbie was gone. And Deborah was back. He saw her straighten her shoulders, take a deep breath, and in a voice that quavered just a little, she asked,

'Is there anything you need me to do Mr Stewart? I've finished sorting out the filing.'

He paused, trying to take it all in. For a brief moment her composure slipped and he could see tears beginning to form in her tired eyes.

'Just some letters, please, Deborah. I've made my usual notes.'

He handed the bundle to her. As their eyes met, she gave a brief nod of acknowledgement. He cleared his throat. 'Welcome back, Deborah. I'm sure we'll be a great team.'

Back in his office he drew the calendar out of the drawer. His lovely Debbie was there, with a delighted-looking Mr Prendergast. She was turned slightly, facing out of the picture. And she was captured in mid-wink. He grinned and winked back. Then noticed the caption. 'A good secretary is always there when you need her.' Well, Debbie would stay on his wall till the end of the year but maybe, after that, he could keep her somewhere safe. Just in case of need.

A Light in Time

Wiping sweat from her brow with the back of one hand, Kelly trailed disconsolately down the track, following Ben. Her sandals scuffed in the dust as she dragged her feet. A plastic bag dangled from her other wrist. On it in lurid colours was the legend 'Benvenuti a Pompeii', above a picture of the volcano. It wasn't that she hadn't wanted to come on the trip. She'd enjoyed most of it. In fact she'd felt quite emotional seeing evidence of lives stopped so dramatically, learning all about the terrible eruption that had buried an entire town for so long. And knowing that the streets she walked along were the very ones where Roman citizens had strolled. Pompeii was a tragedy frozen in time. There had been one or two moments, when everything was quiet and other tourists had moved ahead, that the past had seemed so real, so close, she felt as though she could almost see it, hear it, touch it. There had been that sensation of something at the corner of her vision. A slight hint of other sounds covered by the breeze. She had felt somehow *connected* with the past.

No, Pompeii was okay. The problem was with Ben. He wasn't just interested in a touristy kind of way, but in a nerdy got-to-go-into-every-little-detail way. And quite frankly Kelly had seen enough culture for one day. Having completed the walking tour through the ruins they'd got as far as the souvenir shop where she had browsed happily for a while before buying postcards and some little candles in glass jars engraved with 'Pompeii'. Ben had scoffed at this.

'Oh for pete's sake, Kelly, you can buy candles anywhere. If you have to get something why not have one or two of those clay lamps? At least they're reproductions of real things the Romans used.'

But Kelly pointed out that *they* weren't scented with lavender and patchouli, though she did slip one into her shopping. It was in a kit with a little plastic container of oil and a cotton wick. She added a small lighter when she saw them displayed by the till, thinking she might try to make it work later on. Her little brother had been very excited about 'doing the Romans' at school so maybe he'd like to see a copy of an everyday object they had used.

As she queued to pay, her thoughts were on getting back to the hotel and finding a shady spot by the pool. It was early afternoon and the August heat was intense. She was visualising a cooling dip, followed by a doze under an umbrella. Unfortunately that was when Ben had wandered outside and got into conversation with the American guy he introduced to her as Brett. It seemed Brett was working on a dig with a team of students from Bologna University. He explained how the work on the area of Pompeii known as Porta Stabia had been going on for years and was still far from finished.

'It was a relatively poor area, so we're finding out about the lives of the less well-off inhabitants ...'

Ben was enthralled and asked question after question, all quite technical stuff about the actual process of archaeological investigations, until Brett said he could perhaps show them a small part of the dig. Of course, Ben had leapt at the chance. So now they were back on the site, hurrying across the uneven ground to get there 'while the rest of them have stopped for lunch'. Leaving Kelly to dawdle reluctantly behind them.

****

Marcia struggled with the wooden door. She had been so sure that was father's voice, calling for help, and had tried to push the door open to let him in. Not only was father not outside, but the tiny gap she'd manage to force open showed her how high the ash and pumice stones were piling against the other side. Horrified she had tried to pull it shut again but couldn't quite manage it. Tiny shards of rock had caught beneath the wood and were wedging it open. It wasn't a huge gap, but already the ash was forcing its way in much faster than before and she was sure she could feel the heat rise even more rapidly in the little house. Before father had wrapped his cloak around his head and ventured outside to find out what was happening, he had told her on no account to open the door until his return. It had been stifling inside. Now it was worse. The air was already thick with dust and smoke, making it hard to breathe and there were terrible noises outside. Where was father? He had said he wouldn't be long but that was ages ago. At least, it felt like ages. It was hard to tell what time of day it was. Surely the sky should be bright by now? But instead everywhere was filled with the terrible blackness. Even inside, the air was choked with swirling dust. It crunched beneath her feet. Her eyes streamed with the grit. And the heat had a dryness to it that seared her lungs.

Marcia tried so hard not to give in to weeping but it was awful being alone like this. She feared she would die, caught in here. And, even worse, that she would die alone. She prayed hard inside her head for Vesta, goddess of hearth and home, to remember this household and save her. There was no answer. She was gasping for air now but forced herself to make her way across to the lalarium, the tiny altar shelf on the wall next to the hearth. Perhaps her prayers would be heard more easily in the place dedicated to the gods. To her horror she realised the little lamp set there was no longer burning. No wonder the gods were not helping her! Father had lit the lucerna when the mountain had started to erupt and they had prayed together for deliverance, for the eruption to end, for the town to be saved. She groped for the lamp and saw that it still had oil. Why had it gone out? Ash continued to fall in relentless torrents outside the door but mixed in with it were rocks, some burning as they fell. Forced almost to the floor by lack of air, choking in spite of the cloth she had pulled over her nose and mouth, she held the wick through the gap and against a burning rock. It browned immediately and began to smoke then flare but as she pulled it back the flame died out. She realised there was not enough air left to feed the flame. Heartbroken and terrified, knowing that if the flame could not survive nor could she, Marcia collapsed onto the floor. She began to drag herself across the floor, praying all the time for the gods to be with her, not to leave her alone. A few feet from the door, suffocating, she was forced to stop. There she lay, her head stretched back searching for a glimpse of the altar through the deepening murk.

****

Ben and Brett had stopped at the side of one of the many trenches.

'This would have been a small household, you can see the extent of the walls….just a couple of rooms… a hearth set here ….'

Kelly caught them up as Brett was explaining what they could see. There was a mound on the floor. Slowly she began to make sense of the shape, that of a huddled figure, one arm stretched over its head, away from them. It almost seemed to be pointing.

'What do you think this person was doing in that position?' she asked.

'Who knows,' Brett replied. 'We are pretty sure though that she's a girl. Quite young, judging from her size.'

It seemed awfully sad that this young girl should have died alone in this place. Where was her family? And the position she was in somehow gave a sense of yearning, of need. As though she were stretching out her arm for someone. Kelly would have liked to ask more about the girl but didn't want Ben to start teasing about her over-active imagination.

Brett continued describing the things they knew about how a house of this sort would have been furnished, how the inhabitants probably lived, and she stood half listening to his account, half wondering what the poor girl's final moments had been like. But when he described the altar shelf and how the Romans worshipped their gods, a vivid picture sprang into her mind. It was as if she could just see it. The gods, that's who the girl was reaching for. If you were all alone at such a frightening time, you'd call upon whatever you believed in to help you, to be with you. It made sense to Kelly. Silently she sent out a prayer of her own. I hope you were there for her. I hope she found some comfort.

'There would probably have been a small lamp, a lucerna, that would be lit for special rites. Perhaps morning and evening ....'
She reached in her bag for the lamp kit.

'Is this the sort of thing you mean?'

'Yes,' said Brett, pleased that she was taking an interest, 'here, let me show you.'

He jumped down into the cleared area and set up the lamp on the ground, filling it with oil and fitting the wick. Kelly begged him to light it and passed him the lighter she'd bought. He laughed at her eagerness.

'It's not going to shine very brightly against this sunlight!'

But he humoured her and lit the lamp, then held it at shoulder height.

'This is about where it would have been.....'

Kelly didn't know why she had felt it so important to see the lamp lit but as the tiny flame took hold a feeling of rightness washed over her. For just a moment or two she felt a sense of peace, of oneness.

****

There was a crushing pain in Marcia's chest and her eyes began to close but as she dragged one last tiny gasp of hot air into her lungs, a miracle happened. Ahead of her, through the dreadful dark, a lamp shone brightly. She stretched out her hand towards it. Despite the thickly choked air it seemed to blaze up, brighter and brighter.

As the life faded from her body she knew that her prayers had been answered. A light shone out for her. It shone brightly, just in time.

Sweet William

It was a sad day for Dot when she and Bill moved out of their little terraced house and into a one-bedroom bungalow in a sheltered housing complex. Sad because it meant leaving behind the little garden that Dot had created over the thirty odd years they had lived there. It was her little patch of heaven, she would tell everyone, and she loved to show people around. She knew all the names of the plants, their Latin and common versions, and reckoned no plant was beyond her abilities. Bill often said she could plant a walking stick and something would grow and flower from it. Sometimes over the years he'd grumble about the time she wasted outside but, as she was quick to point out, he was happy to spend hours in front of the tv watching a load of daft men kicking a ball about. At least she was outside, breathing the fresh air and getting some exercise. For some time though she hadn't been able to get out much and now that she was confined to a wheelchair they had to move to somewhere more manageable.

Once the move was over Dot got restless. Sitting still just didn't feel right.

'All that grass outside the window,' she'd say, 'but not a plant or flower to look at.'

'Well it's all communal, isn't it?' said Bill. 'And it's probably cheaper to send someone round with a sit-on mower every few weeks than pay for a gardener.'

She knew he was right but still itched to tend her plants again. So slowly over the next few weeks pots began to appear in their tiny living room. At first there were one or two given as housewarming presents. Then an occasional one that she would insist on buying from the supermarket when Bill pushed her round to get their shopping. Bit by bit word got around that if you had a plant that was ailing Dot could nurse it back to health. And a 'hospital wing' sprang up along the kitchen windowsill. Other people would pop round to visit and bring a cutting for her. More pots appeared in the bedroom and even in the bathroom. Bill told anyone who would listen that there wasn't any room to rest so much as a mug of tea, every surface was taken up with plants. Still, he understood how much they meant to her and knowing how frail she was getting, he tried not to complain too much.

Eventually Dot's health had deteriorated to such an extent that she spent most of her time in bed. Unless one of the nurses called in Bill wasn't able to lift her in or out of bed. And she no longer had the strength to help in supporting her own weight. Not that she weighed so much anymore. Bill would help her wash each day and worried that she was disappearing before his eyes. If only she could get out and about a bit again it might give her the incentive to keep going as long as possible. They'd been promised a hoist but there was a waiting list. So there she lay directing all plant care from her bed while Bill pottered about, seeing to the plants' needs as well as those of his wife. He tried not to let her see how very afraid he was that he might soon lose her. He couldn't even begin to think how he could cope without his Dottie.

All their married life they'd covered up their love for each other with a kind of gruffness, making jokes that might have shocked some but which provided coded messages to each other. When Dot said she'd didn't think she'd be around much longer and Bill replied, 'I should be so lucky! If they ever carted you off you'd be back to haunt me in no time. You just wouldn't be able to stand seeing me get on so well', what they were actually doing was trying to voice their fears about the impending separation. Sometimes in a quiet moment Dot would rest one of her thin frail hands on Bill's and say in a subdued voice, 'You're a good man Bill. Don't think I don't appreciate everything you do.' And he would shrug off her comment with some sharp reply, 'Don't go getting all soft on me!' but he would place his free hand on top of hers and pat it gently before heading to the kitchen to put the kettle on.

Each morning he would wake with a start and just lie there with his eyes closed trying to hear if Dot was breathing. Once he'd made sure she was still with him he'd allow himself to wake up properly and get on with the day, feeling as though he'd had a reprieve. But as time went on his relief at having her there was tinged with distress at the pain and discomfort she was in. The nurses were calling more frequently now, doing things that he was glad he didn't have to know too much about, but there was a limit to how much they could help. His poor Dottie was hanging on to life despite her pain and eventually he began to suspect that it was only for him that she forced herself to stay.

There came a day when she had been so low he'd sat beside her bed most of the day, afraid to leave her for more than a minute. Eventually she had said in a quiet voice,

'Oh Bill, I'm so tired of this. I wish the two of us were sitting in my garden together.'

Bill felt his heart was breaking in two but he held her hand and said,

'You know, I reckon if there are gardens anywhere, there'll be gardens in heaven. If you need to go Dot, don't hang about for me. It's all right,'

She smiled at him then closed her eyes, saying 'You know I would never leave you, don't you?'

She slept for a while and Bill nodded off beside her, still holding onto her. Sometime that evening, while he was unaware, she slipped gently away.

The days and weeks that followed were terrible for Bill. He couldn't bear to see all the plants around the bungalow. Without Dot's regular reminders and instructions they were no longer thriving and he knew how upset she'd be at their loss. One by one he gave them away to friends and neighbours, Without Dot, without Dot's plants, the place seemed so empty. He wished with all his heart she *would* come back and haunt him.

'I'd like that, Dot,' he whispered looking at her photo. 'we made a good team, you and me. All those years.... It just doesn't work, being on my own like this.'

The warden of the complex was worrying about Bill. Some of his neighbours had spoken to her about him too, and she in turn had spoken to Bill's doctor.

'The best thing,' he had said, 'would be to get him engaged in some activity. Get him out of that place occasionally.'

Now, after a lot of ideas she'd had to discard as being unlikely to help, she thought she'd come up with a good one but it would take a bit of organising. There would need to be some funding. Over the next few weeks she got a few of the more active residents involved in some money-raising activities – a cake sale and then a jumble sale – and managed to get a grant from one of the charities that support the elderly. Then when everything was in place she broached the matter with Bill. A small patch of the communal gardens (just grass, as Dot had pointed out), was directly in front of his home. As his was at the end of the row nobody walked along there, and nobody but Bill needed access. She proposed that he should make it into a little garden, in memory of Dot. She had raised enough money for plants and a little bench to sit out on. Maybe a bird table or whatever he thought… Of course, Bill had protested that he couldn't possibly. His wife had been the one with all the gardening skills. He wouldn't even know what to plant.

'There are books,' she had pointed out, 'and it would be a lovely memorial for Dot.'

There certainly were books. Still on the bookcase, from before Dot's illness. Having grudgingly said he'd think about it, Bill found himself filling one or two lonely evenings reading some of them. The pictures were certainly beautiful. He'd got in mind roses… Dot always loved roses…

'There's a rose for every situation,' she'd said. 'Climbers, ramblers, scented, miniature. And just about every colour. You can have early-flowering ones and others that go right up to winter.'

Maybe it wouldn't be too difficult to look after a garden if it only contained one type of plant. 'I'll do it,' he told the warden, much to her delight. So she arranged to give him a lift to the nearest garden centre. There a young lad was assigned to wheel a trolley around and lift onto it any plants Bill selected. They would all be delivered to the complex along with bags of compost and feed, once Bill and some of the stronger residents had prepared the ground for them. They spent their time in the rose section. Bill tried to get one of every variety that caught his eye. He went for different colours and different habits. He didn't bother with trying to read the tiny print on the labels. The young lad was able to tell him what colour each one would be, when it would flower and for how long, and how it liked to be grown. He had to wheel the trolley away at one point and come back with an empty one.

By the time they'd got to the checkout the man in charge of the garden centre had been made aware of the memorial garden project. He had managed to get a local newspaper to send along a reporter with a camera to take a picture and they posed together in front of the trolleys. Ever mindful of the effect of good publicity, the manager insisted on donating some plants as a 'gift' from the centre. Bill started to point out that it was to be a rose garden, and even he could tell these weren't roses, but it was as if he could hear Dot whispering, 'Never look a gift horse in the mouth, Bill'. So he kept quiet and accepted them.

Two days later the plants were delivered. They stood in a line awaiting Bill's decision about where to put them. Fetching his reading glasses and a notepad and pencil, he decided to be methodical. He would write down all the names as a record then when they were planted he'd do some painted wooden name signs to stand at the foot of each one. Laboriously he wrote down the names in a list. The free gift plants were first. 'Dianthus barbatus', he read. 'Can't be doing with that. He found the common name underneath and wrote that down. 'English names'll do,' he said to himself.

And so the list read:

Sweet William

Super Star

Super Hero

My Valentine

Best Friend

Close to You

Scent from Above

In Appreciation

Thank You

Remember Me

Dorothy Goodwin

The last name quite startled him. Dot's name before they married was Dorothy Goldwin – almost the same! He was so pleased he'd put it on the trolley. How thrilled she would have been to see that name. He glanced up and down the list. So strange that it started with a reference to his name – William – then ended with Dot. He couldn't have planned it better. He started to read the list aloud but partway through his voice faltered.

'Well I never ... Oh Dottie, you've only gone and done it, haven't you!'

For there in front of him was the clearest love letter anyone ever received. He'd got it wrong again it seemed. Instead of making a garden to tell Dottie how he felt about her she'd turned the tables and used it to talk to him instead.

It took a while to plant everything and Bill made sure he kept the plants in the order of Dot's message. When anyone came to wander through his 'little patch of heaven' they could read the letter from the labels he marked up. And when Bill sat out among the roses he never felt alone. He knew his Dottie was still there, keeping an eye on him, and he would chat quietly to her. 'Not too loudly, mind,' he told her, 'or someone'll hear and they'll cart me off to the funny farm.' He suspected her green fingers were still working their magic too, for in spite of his lack of know-how everything in the little garden took and flourished. Trust Dot to have the last word.

Nineteen Eighty Five

Zoe sat in her bedsit staring at the money she had scattered across the bedcover. It was freezing in the room but she couldn't turn on the heat. Not if she was going to eat for the rest of the week. And get to and from work. She thought there was a chance she could scrounge a lift as far as the town centre most evenings, and then it would be possible to walk the rest of the way. She sighed. How come she ended up in this state every month? It wasn't as though she'd been living in the lap of luxury. Okay, so there had been four Friday nights which had involved a fair amount of drinking, but she hadn't had to pay for *all* her drinks. Dev from accounts had been there. She'd bought a couple of gorgeous tops to wear and a pair of boots. But boots are really an essential in the winter, aren't they? She sighed again. She had exactly nineteen pounds eighty-five pence to see her through till the end of the month. Nineteen eighty-five. The year she was born – what a coincidence.

She moved £5 across the bedspread. That would cover her fares one way. She would just have to shiver each morning without heating. Then if she put aside another £10 she could have enough electricity to take the chill off the room in the evening and cook something quick on her one-ring baby cooker, beans on toast or a bowl of soup. Perhaps after that she could pile a few coats and other clothes on the bed and crawl in. Some early nights might not be a bad thing. That left – she frowned – four pounds eighty-five pence for anything else she needed.

She checked over her food stock. Two small tins of spaghetti hoops and one large tin of beans. She wondered if she would have the nerve to scrounge a few meals from her mum, then realised it would cost her more to get back from there than to buy some food. Besides, twenty-six years old, and she was still thinking about heading home to mum! After all the things she'd said. Well, yelled. About needing her independence. About being stifled. About how she could manage perfectly well on her own. And, no, she wouldn't come crawling back any time soon. Truth was she'd always had a tricky relationship with her mum. And after dad died it seemed to bring the worst out in both of them. Her mum believed that as long as Zoe was living in *her* house, living off *her* income, then she should do as she was told. Zoe knew her dad would never have gone along with that. He'd always indulged his only daughter.

'Ah, come on, Beth,' he used to say, 'give the poor girl some space. While she's young she should be enjoying herself.' And when mum wasn't looking he'd give Zoe a crafty wink and slip a few notes into her hand. She missed that easy-going kindness.

Mum's life had been much tougher, as she made a point of telling Zoe at every opportunity. Nagging at her constantly. She laid down strict rules on just about everything. Scarcely a day went by without the words 'While you're living in my house you'll…' escaping from her lips. And the more she'd treated her daughter like a child, the more Zoe had wanted to behave like one. Slamming doors. Sulking. Needing dozens of reminders to get out of bed and off to work. Expecting washing to miraculously clean itself, just like the dishes and mugs left piled in the sink and abandoned. Or under the bed till mould grew on them. And once Beth lost her husband things got even more difficult. With only her wages coming in she needed Zoe to make a contribution. Both financial and practical. She sat Zoe down to talk through the situation but her daughter was having none of it.

'I'm planning to move out,' she announced, cutting her mother off in mid-flow, although until that moment she'd had no plans at all. 'It's about time I got a place of my own.' Of course, mum had told her she'd never manage on the amount she was earning. 'Then I guess I'll have to learn,' she'd announced airily. And from then on it just went downhill until they were both yelling the kind of things that are very hard to take back once they're out of your mouth. She left 'for good' a couple of days later and in all the months she had been away she had only phoned home a couple of times, and hadn't visited at all, in spite of being just a few miles away. Her mother had left messages on her mobile. She'd written a couple of short letters. She'd even tried sending text messages. At first Zoe had ignored all the attempts to keep in touch because she still felt angry with her mum. When she started to admit to herself that she may have been a bit hasty and her mum may have been partly right, it was too late. Pride kept her from letting on just how difficult things were.

She looked around her bedsit. God, what a dump. When she first moved in she'd had all these grand plans about making it look really cool. Grown-up, modern, but with a twist of individuality. She'd pored over pictures in magazines and fantasised about her new home. Never *did* any of it. Money just didn't stretch far enough. Not if she was going to have some sort of social life as well. And she wasn't the cleanest or tidiest of people without someone picking up after her.

Now here she was on a Sunday evening, stuck inside, wondering how she was going to make it to Friday's payday. And less than a fiver to live off. She gathered up the money, pulled on a coat and stuffed the cash in her pocket, grabbed a crumpled carrier bag from under the heap of washing lying in the corner, and headed off to the nearest convenience store. As she piled items into the basket she kept a count under her breath. It would be mortifying to have the total rung up and then admit to not having the money. Nobody would believe that she just hadn't brought enough cash with her. Everyone used plastic these days. Actually that was what she would like to do but she'd already maxed out two cards and had received threatening letters about paying it all back. She'd had to go to the bank and set up a couple of direct debits to pay back an agreed amount each month. She knew if she defaulted just once her agreement with the two companies would be void and there'd be serious consequences. That, of course, was another reason she couldn't make her salary stretch each month. She was carrying a load of debt from before. Looking back, she wasn't sure what she'd actually spent it all on. Apart from the holiday in Corfu. Mostly it had just trickled through her fingers and now she owed thousands. That had all been back when she first moved out. When she was still grieving for her dad but she'd sort of lost her mum and home too. There had been a fair amount of spending to compensate for the losses she felt.

One carton of milk. She didn't have a fridge but there was a spot just outside her window where she could balance it on a ledge. In this weather it should keep easily. One small piece of the cheapest cheese. A tub of spread. Two large loaves. She stopped, put back the cheese, too expensive. Ditto the spread. She went to the corner where soon-to-out-of-date food was marked down. There she got a couple of slightly-dented tins of soup and spotted a small tube of squeezy cheese. Only seventy pence, and she could scrape it on the bread thinly. That would do for lunches. She headed off to the small queue that had formed. Adding up her shopping as she stood waiting she realised it was exactly a pound less than she carried in her pocket. Another little coincidence, she thought. Even though she'd checked over and over, she still held her breath as her few items were beeped through the till.

'Three pounds eighty-five, please.'

She was holding her cash ready and took out a one-pound coin before handing over the rest. The young lad serving her laboured over counting it before giving her a cursory nod and turning to drop the money in. Before she knew what she was saying, she proffered her last coin and said, 'And I'll take one of those scratchcards, please.'

She walked out of the shop, dropping her receipt and the scratchcard in her bag. 'Idiot, idiot, *idiot*,' went the voice in her head. Her last pound and she'd thrown it away on one of those stupid cards. Why? She didn't usually buy them. Her mum had always said they were 'a mug's game'. Somehow, standing in the queue, the display on the counter had caught her eye. All those pound signs. And the thought that maybe, with a little bit of luck, she might win something...

Back in her room she made herself a mug of tea and a few slices of dry toast. Then turned off everything, including the light, to save what little electricity was still on the meter. She sat huddled in just about every item of clothing she owned, with the curtain open as she tried to read an old magazine by the orange glow of the streetlight just along from her window. Eventually she gave up and crawled into bed, feeling the lowest and saddest she could remember being since her dad died.

Next morning her room was like the inside of a fridge. Her nose was so cold she couldn't feel it and she shivered as she had a quick strip-wash then fumbled her way into her clothes. Thank goodness it was a weekday and she could sit in a nice warm office once she got to work. There was a tea and coffee machine for the customers to use as they waited, but no-one minded if staff made occasional use of it. Especially if they were making a drink for a customer at the same time. If she was careful who was on duty in the front office, she could keep topping up with hot drinks through the day. Next to the complimentary drinks there was a little basket of cheap biscuits, each pair sealed in cellophane. She usually disdained them – they tasted like sweet cardboard – but she thought she could stock up on those too, eating some and slipping some more in her bag for home. Her mind skipped about as she sat sorting invoices. No money left for things like toilet rolls but they were a bit too bulky for 'borrowing' from work. Maybe if she unrolled some each time she used the ladies' she could fold it up small enough to put down the inside of her boot and by the time she'd got home there'd be enough. She had already arranged a lift to the town after work.

'Off shopping for clothes, again?' her colleague had asked. She didn't contradict, just grinned and said, 'Maybe I'll just have a look, see what's on offer.' Sam's mum had been baking so she had a couple of chunks of sponge cake in with her lunch. She offered one to Zoe who took it gratefully. Not that she let the gratitude show on her face. Just say a casual, 'Oh, yeah, thanks. I didn't get up too early today so I didn't have time to pack much.' As she munched it she carried on planning her survival strategy for the rest of the week. Once she got to the town centre that evening she could pop into the library for an hour or two. They kept it nice and toasty for the kids and pensioners. And she could pop in and see if they were giving away tasters in the supermarket. For a moment she considered stealing some food in there but once her imagination put up a film of her getting caught, the humiliation, the picture on the front page of her local newspaper, she decided she didn't have the temperament for major crime. Taking a few bits and pieces from work didn't matter though, she thought, and she got home with a bag stuffed full of rolled up toilet paper, a soap refill she could use if she took the top off, a load of biscuits and some drinks sachets. Plus a slightly wrinkly apple from more affluent times, that she'd found in her desk drawer. Coming up the communal stairs to her room she'd spotted a twenty pence piece lying in a dusty corner of the landing and had picked it up. It joined the little pile she'd put together for electricity and bus fares. 'Every little helps,' she muttered.

Another dreary evening stretched ahead. No tv. That had gone back when she got into debt with the credit cards. No mp3 player. She'd sold that at the same time. And she'd read every bit of paper in the room. Disconsolately she started picking up clothes and sorting them into piles for hanging up or shoving in the laundry bag. Right at that moment it would have felt like the height of luxury to be able to take her dirty things down to the laundrette, feed coins into the machine, and sit in the warm watching it go round and round. The bag of shopping lay where she had left it and she rummaged in it for a tin of soup to heat. That was when she spotted the scratchcard. Well, that might while away a few seconds of her evening. Picking up the twenty pence coin she had found she started to rub off the blocks of silver. It was a Fruit Machine card – three symbols the same and it meant you had won the amount next to them.

Two cherries and a lemon. Huh. One cherry, one bunch of grapes and an orange. Another huh. Three oranges. Huh.

She almost tossed the card away as a reflex action, having absolutely no expectation of a win. Then her brain registered the fact that she really had seen three identical symbols. She started to scratch away at the amount box, and nearly shouted out loud as a five appeared. £5 would double the amount she had to live on. Plus it would be a £4 profit on buying the card. Then as a nought appeared and she could see she'd won £50 she felt as though everything in her world had come right. But the noughts continued to appear as she scratched. In utter disbelief she saw the numbers grow. £50... £500... £5000... £50000. Fifty thousand pounds! The room tipped crazily around her and she had to sit taking deep breaths as the pounding in her chest slowly subsided. Wow! She looked again, scarcely daring to believe she'd got it right, but under the numbers in small print was written FIFTY THOUSAND. It was real. She had won fifty thousand pounds. She kept repeating the number over and over. Eventually she settled into a stunned silence while she thought it through.

Her first instinct was to run around telling everyone she met about her good fortune. Instead she raided her travel and heating money and took her currently unusable phone down to the local shop and paid for a top-up. Back in her room she telephoned the number on the back of the scratchcard and was soon through to a very pleasant-sounding woman who took her details and the code from the card. Having checked with her computer she confirmed the win and put Zoe through to an adviser.

'Obviously with *larger* wins…'

She doesn't think this is a large win? Zoe was astounded.

'…we talk through such things as privacy options. Here, it's entirely up to you what you say. Your name will not be published by us, nor do we give out information to the media. We can suggest a financial adviser, if you would like one. As for payment of the money, we can dispatch payment by courier or, if you care to give us your bank details, we can arrange a direct transfer electronically.'

'Which is quicker?' Her voice came out a little squeaky with excitement and tension.

'The direct transfer. You will have to check with your bank as every one of them seems to allow different times to acknowledge the amount is there. Once it's cleared you can do as you like with it.'

'Thank you so much,' Zoe stuttered out, once her information had been put into the system.

'No problem. I do hope you enjoy your win.'

After the call she sat on her bed feeling dazed. It would be great to go out and celebrate but she didn't have the cash. Instead she fed most of the remainder of her money into the meter, got the room cosy, and made tea and toast. Then she started to make plans. A croaky-voiced call to Sam with a suggestion that she 'might be coming down with something' got her a promise to 'let the boss know', and the next day off. She would head to the bank and find out when the money was there.

She decided her first priority was to pay off her credit card debts. With interest it had piled up to seventeen thousand. Without that she would feel a whole lot freer. Then... oh, wow, it just had to be a car. Dad had started teaching her to drive when she was seventeen, and when that wasn't too successful had paid for lessons for her. It had taken two goes to pass, with her mum sniffing disapprovingly in the background and complaining about the waste of money. 'Even if you could afford to buy a car on what you earn, you wouldn't be able to afford to run one. Have you any idea how much the insurance would be for a girl your age?'

That was so like her mum, always throwing cold water on everything. Dad would have put his hand straight in his pocket, insisting on helping her out. Well now she could afford a car, and afford to run it and insure it. And the first place she would go would be back to her mum's for a visit, just so she could show off how well she was doing. That was when she decided the win would be her secret. She could hardly show off to her mum if it was all down to a win on a scratchcard. She'd pretend to be managing really well on her money and saving up for things. That would do it.

The next morning she explained to a disinterested cahier that she was expecting a 'large sum' to arrive in her account. And how long would it take? It was transferred yesterday. The girl told her she would check her account. She tapped a few keys but just said, 'You have less than £10 in your account.' She supposed it might show on the account after 11am as there would have been a system update by then. Fidgety with nerves, excitement, and a dragging anxiety that maybe it was all a mistake, Zoe took herself off to a nearby café and used even more of her rapidly vanishing reserve of cash to buy herself a latte. She lingered over it for as long as she could then braved the cold and wandered up and down the street, looking in shop windows and fantasising about walking in and buying anything she wanted. She left it till twenty past eleven before going back to the bank again. Same cashier. Same disinterested response. Then, as she checked the account, the girl's body language underwent a subtle shift.

She looked up from her computer screen, a pleasant smile on her face,

'Yes, Miss Vincent, a deposit of fifty thousand pounds has been made to your account and is available to you. It's rather a large amount for an instant access account, but I can call through an adviser to explain about our...'

'No thank you,' Zoe interrupted. 'I have plans for the money.'

She passed over payment slips for her two credit cards and said grandly,

'I'd like to pay these please. In full. And then I'd like to withdraw two hundred pounds in cash.'

The cashier seemed disappointed. Maybe she was on a commission for selling the banks' other products? Tough. Zoe wasn't biting. After the slips were stamped and passed back, she swept out of the bank, head held high. She stopped at the taxi rank, clambered gratefully into the back seat of a warm cab, and rode in style to the large car dealership on the outskirts of the town. Her new life was about to begin.

When she arrived she had every intention of buying a reconditioned, secondhand car but was quickly won over by the salesman's patter and found herself looking at brand new cars instead. 'You could drive this little beauty away today,' he enthused. The sign on the car roof claimed she could 'Drive away for £12 999 – including a year's tax and free accessories'. The salesman took her out for a test drive. He drove at first, then they swapped seats. She explained nervously that it had been a while since she'd driven – in fact it was a couple of years. Dad used to let her borrow the car in the evenings but after he died the car was one of the first things mum got rid of. Zoe had kicked up a major fuss about that. She was sure dad would have wanted her to have it. Now she stalled the car once or twice, and lurched up the road. But the salesman didn't seem to notice or mind. 'That's great!' he said encouragingly, 'you soon got the hang of this one. Lovely car to drive, isn't it? So easy for parking too.'

She had to agree. Once back on the forecourt she was whisked inside for a cup of coffee and to discuss options. She hadn't even realised she'd made a decision. Before she knew it, she was signing papers and handing over her bank card. Of course, it would take a few hours to 'process the payment' which she understood to mean 'check you've actually got the money in your account'. And the £12 999 soon changed once vat was added on. And then there were the 'customised features' the salesman pointed out in the brochure. In for a penny and all that. Yes, she'd love the heated seat. And the special little mats. And the upgrade to the music system. And the parking sensors. But knowing she had fifty thousand pounds made Zoe a little blasé about spending, and in truth it had all gone to her head a bit. The salesman, 'Terry, please, ...' even gave her a lift back to town so she could have lunch and do a bit of shopping, promising to call her on the mobile as soon as her car was ready to collect. He pointed out where she could arrange insurance too, something she'd forgotten to factor in. Ah well, fifty thousand is fifty thousand.

Over the next two weeks she was in a complete whirl. It was like being some kind of super hero. By day, an ordinary office worker. By night, the girl about town. It was a good job the shops stayed open so late. Her room was now repainted with a feature wall of very expensive paper. She giggled to herself as she pictured her mum's face at the thought of spending a hundred and twenty pounds on one roll of wallpaper! Zoe didn't do the work of course.

She paid the guy who rented the room above her. Most of her old furniture and belongings headed straight to the local tip, via the boot of her new car. She had been to the nicest shops for her new bed that folded up to the wall. It made the room look so much better during the day. Then there were lamps and side tables, pictures on the wall. She even managed to fit a small cooker in to her cooking corner along with an Italian coffee machine. There was a fancy flatscreen tv on the wall, a games console, a new mp3 player, plus a top of the range speaker system that was so small and discreet you'd hardly know it was there. That item alone cost the best part of a thousand, but it was such good quality. She bought a laptop and arranged a wifi connection. And a cable tv package. She upgraded her pay-as-you-go mobile to a smart phone. Her tiny closet space was bursting at the seams with designer label clothes, shoes, bags. It was AMAZING how much you could fit into one room. She almost wished she'd got a bigger place to live but didn't think the money would stretch quite that far. She had also thought of giving up her job, but common-sense kept her from that too. Although there had been some very expensive nights out. A fancy restaurant. A new club. With Zoe always first to the bar to buy the drinks. It wasn't just Sam who came with her. They had a loose-knit group of friends around, none they knew particularly well, but who were always ready to party. Especially if someone else would be covering the bill.

Zoe felt she was finally living the kind of life she should have had all along. If her dad hadn't died so unexpectedly. If she had still been living at home, her salary treated as her own fun money, her parents subsidising her. She remembered the plan to swagger back for a visit and grinned. Maybe this weekend.

A few more months drifted by. She booked a two-week Caribbean cruise for herself. And, since she didn't want to go alone, paid for Sam to accompany her. Her friend was shocked at such generosity but Zoe let her think she'd inherited some money from her dad, and that she'd got the cabin as an on-line bargain.

'Even so,' said Sam, 'it must be costing more than every other holiday I've had put together! Are you *sure*?' She must have asked that a dozen times but her friend always reassured her.

'You know my motto – if you've got it, enjoy it!'

Zoe felt a slight pang of conscience and made a quick phone call to her mum before flying out with Sam to join the ship. She mentioned that she would be going away but her mum went on about 'affording it' and 'I hope you're living within your means'. That stung, so she cut the call short without saying where she would be going. If she'd stopped to think she would have realised her uncomfortable feelings arose from the fact that her mum was right about her. She didn't live within her means. Never had. And it was just the luck of the win that enabled her to hold her head up and pretend she could cope. Somewhere at the back of her mind she filed away a thought about getting to grips with her finances once she got back. She really ought to think about investing or saving some of the money. Then she forgot about all of it, and set her mind on enjoying the trip. Once on board the cruise ship everything was included but she still managed to run through a few hundred pounds picking up 'souvenirs'. She sent a postcard of the Bahamas to her mum, wishing she could see her face when she got it.

It was a fantastic holiday and they arrived back in England glowing with sun and some wonderful memories. But, back at work again, Zoe realised how boring she found her job. Maybe she could use some of her money to set up a small business? She started reading a few specialist magazines, looking for information and ideas. Maybe she could buy a franchise of some kind. She looked at some that attracted her – mostly to do with beauty products or lingerie - but soon understood they were beyond her. Fifty thousand was a lot but it couldn't buy everything. She remembered her quiet promise to sort out finances and decided to work on it that very weekend. She knew she'd spent some of the win but hadn't really reckoned up how much. She'd go through all the paperwork. See how things stood.

So that Saturday she lifted down the pile of unopened envelopes from the top shelf, where she tended to throw them. She could see which ones were from the credit card companies but hadn't realised there would be so many. It was a pleasure to open them and find nothing to pay. No interest to be charged. But they weren't all statements. There were letters from both of them arranging to increase her spending limit. Or offering 'instant cheques' that would let her draw cash from her cards. They'd even printed some and posted them to her. She was absolutely shocked by this. They knew she had got into trouble with repayments yet, as soon as she was clear of debt, they were offering her even more opportunities to get into debt again. It was like buying an alcoholic a bottle of whisky. She was so outraged she felt like writing back and telling them what she thought of their business 'ethics', then realised that this was something for her to deal with. She got the scissors out, cut up their letters, cheques and her own cards, put the pieces in two envelopes

– their envelopes, postage paid ones – and then popped out and put them in the letterbox down the road. No more credit, she told herself firmly.

Back in her room she was rummaging through for the bank statements when she noticed a letter with her mum's writing on it. The postmark was a few days ago. She must have scooped it up and not noticed it. She put it on one side. Bank stuff first, then she see what the letter was about.

Two hours later it was getting dark. She was still sitting there, bank statements gathered in her hands, oblivious to the growing gloom within her bedsit. At first she had told herself it was wrong, there had to be a mistake. She had frantically scribbled a list of everything she had spent since her win. Finally, numb with shock, she had to accept what the bank's information was telling her. Zoe's fifty thousand pounds, her wonderful lucky break, wasn't there anymore. There was less than eight thousand in her account. All the time, as she bought things, the money had stayed at the original amount in her thoughts. She knew she'd spent a lot but somehow had never deducted it in her mind. Less than eight thousand. She'd hoped to use it to change her life but there wasn't really enough for any dramatic change. She couldn't even think about leaving her job. Or travelling abroad for a year. Or opening a little shop. All the ideas she'd had. She had just frittered away the one big bit of luck that was ever likely to come along. Less than eight thousand left. Actually, to be exact, seven thousand and nineteen pounds, eighty-five pence.

It was the nineteen pounds eighty-five that did it. It felt as though she'd almost gone right back to where she started. She felt so angry with herself she started crying. And once started, couldn't stop. She cried for her dad. She cried for the rows with her mum. She cried at her own silliness. She cried at the waste of an opportunity. She cried till the tears dried up and she was left with a stuffy nose and reddened, swollen eyes. Miserably she climbed into bed. Lying in the dark, her thoughts whirling even darker, she eventually drifted off.

When she woke up it was to find her dad tugging on her arm. 'Whaa-a s'amatter?' she asked sleepily, trying to make sense of the situation. Part of her knew there was a reason why dad shouldn't be there, but she couldn't quite figure it out. At the same time, she felt overjoyed to see him. 'Missed you dad,' she mumbled as she struggled to wake. He was standing by the bed now, looking down at her and there was such an expression of love on his face, it made her warm right through. Then she sensed more than love. There was concern too. She knew he wanted to tell her something important. He held a letter in his hand. A letter she knew to be significant. Then he reached for his pockets and slowly pulled them out. They stretched out away from his trousers. He let them go and patted his hands against them. He shrugged and raised his empty hands as if to show her there was nothing in them. A thought crept into her mind. Sorry. So sorry. Zoe slumped back against the pillow, her eyes closing even though she wanted to keep them open. She slept.

The morning sun streamed in through the window. She hadn't pulled the curtains when she went to bed. She rolled over to look at the clock. Half past five! She didn't need to get up for ages. Then she saw the letter from her mum propped up against the box of tissues. Funny. She thought she'd left it with the papers she'd been sorting. Suddenly the discovery of the previous evening jumped back into her mind. But along with it came ... her dad. She'd dreamed about dad. It had seemed so real at the time. She recalled the way he'd patted his pockets. Maybe her dream had been telling her he couldn't be there to help now. No more handouts. Then she remembered the letter he'd been holding. Like the one from her mum. Ah well, better open it and see what she wants.

It had been a very difficult letter to write. Beth had struggled with every word, wanting to bridge the gap with her daughter yet understanding that this letter might drive her further away. But it was time to be honest, to clear the air. And Zoe had to know about the house. After all, it was the only proper home she had ever known.

Dear Zoe,

Thank you for the lovely postcard you sent. I am pleased for you, that you are doing so well. I know it hasn't been easy since Dad died but I reckon he would be proud of how you are getting on. Things have been difficult for me since you left. I hadn't wanted to bother you before but it's got to the point where changes need to be made and I didn't want them to happen behind your back.

First of all I want you to know that I always loved your Dad. I wouldn't have had anyone else, not for anything. He had so many wonderful qualities. But what you probably don't realise is that he was hopeless with money. We'd only been married a few months and I was pregnant with you when I found out just how bad he was at looking after the finances. He'd run up all kinds of debts, and there I was thinking how much it would cost for the pram, and the nappies, and all the rest of it. I kept working till just a few days before you arrived to clear some of it and we agreed, your Dad and I, that I would look after the money from then on. That was all right if I got to his pay packet before anyone else. If someone needed a loan, or he spotted something he wanted to buy for me or you, or if he saw a 'bargain' as he called them, well, the money would be gone and I'd be left wondering how I'd ever manage to feed the three of us. Let alone pay the other bills. And part of his debts was still hanging round our necks like a millstone. That's why I got a job and went back to work when you were still a baby. It kept our heads above water. I paid off those early debts but over the years there'd always be more. He'd come in with that look on his face and I just knew he'd done it again. I don't think he could help it, love, he just never thought through the consequences. He so loved to be generous and open-handed. And he was a sucker for easy loans and buying on credit. All of that sort of thing. I never knew what he was up to till he was in over his head again.

With your Dad being so poorly for those last months, and him not working, things got a bit desperate. That car he'd told us he'd 'bought for a song' from someone at work, well he hadn't. He'd taken out a finance loan for it. And you remember that holiday to Spain he insisted we have as a special time to remember? That was another loan. There was more. A lot more. I didn't know the extent *of it all till he left us. Then I found we owed the best part of fifty thousand. Can you imagine that, Zoe? It's a fortune. For a while I didn't think I'd even have the cash to pay for a decent funeral for your Dad, but Uncle Phil guessed there might be problems – he knew what your Dad was like – and he offered to pay for everything. It was so humiliating knowing we couldn't do it ourselves, but what alternative was there? And I know you wanted your Dad's car love, but it wasn't ours. The finance company repossessed it. At least that was a bit off the debts we owed, though the blasted company still made charges. Can you believe I had to <u>pay</u> them for the privilege of letting them take the car back? That was why I was hoping you'd stay at home and help out a bit with the household expenses. I'd found a second job doing an evening shift over at the garage, just minding the shop really, but there was so much still to pay off. Don't think I'm having a go at you love. You'd only just lost your Dad, I know how painful it all was for you, and you'd got to an age where most sons and daughters want to fly the nest and have a bit of independence. So I do understand and I'm sorry I wasn't honest with you about the situation. I didn't think you needed to hear that sort of thing about your Dad – the two of you were so close. Well, I'm rambling on now. I'm sorry. I'll try to get to the point.*

I've done everything I could love. I've had two jobs going and I took in a lodger after you left, but I haven't made much of a dent in the amount that's still owing. So I'm afraid it's time to let the house go. I've got an agent coming round in a few days. If we can get the house on the market and sell it quickly there'll be time to avoid legal proceedings over the money. It means settling for whatever I can get but there should be enough to cover everything that's owed and buy a small flat somewhere. I've kept all your things for you but I had to put them in boxes and move them out to the shed so the lodger could have your room. But I won't be able to take it all when I move out of here, so would you come and sort through and decide what you want to keep? It'll give you a chance to say your goodbyes to the house. And, of course, I'll get to see you. I have missed you, Zoe, and I'm sorry we parted on bad terms. I just never seem to find the right words with you, the way your Dad did. Please get in touch and come over soon.

With all my love, Mum

Zoe was horrified. A whole lot of things clicked into place. No wonder her Mum always obsessed about money and kept such a tight rein on things. No wonder she worried about Zoe managing. Like father, like daughter. Her dream came back to her. Dad showing his empty pockets, wanting to make her read the letter. The 'sorry' she'd heard in her head. And the coincidence over the amount. To think, she'd won exactly the amount needed to clear Dad's debts, and she'd frittered it away. Poor Mum, sitting on all that worry, trying to get Zoe to pay her way for once. But she had seen it as more evidence of Mum's meanness. Like the car! She was horrified by her own behaviour. Yes, Mum nagged a bit, but given the history... Always protecting Dad from the consequences of his actions. Letting Zoe look up to him as the perfect Dad. When all the time it was Mum left paying the bill for his generosity. Feverishly she cast about for what to do. She still had seven thousand. That might be enough to satisfy creditors and let Mum hold onto the house a bit longer. If she moved back in and added the money she was paying for her room, that would help too. She could use the box-room since there was someone in her bedroom. What else? She thought frantically. Well, there was all this stuff in her room. She could sell it for whatever she could get. She knew from the previous evening that the contents of her room had cost the best part of ten thousand. She supposed she'd be lucky to get half that but it would make a difference. There were specialist shops for designer clothes in good condition. She'd have to check them out online. And there was the car. It had less than a thousand miles on the clock. Maybe she could trade it in for something cheaper.

First though, she needed to speak to her mum. There was no answer when she rang – presumably mum was already at one of her jobs. So she left a message,

'Hi, it's Zoe. I got your letter Mum. I want you to know I'm going to help. Can you put off the estate agent until we've talked things through? I'll come straight over after work tomorrow. About half past six.'

She paused..

'And, Mum, don't worry, we'll work things out. Together. Love you.'

As soon as the car sales place opened, Zoe was there to see about an exchange. 'Terry, Please' wasn't so smiley and accommodating this time. Yes, he could arrange an exchange but Zoe had to realise that a new car depreciates from the moment it's driven off the forecourt. Plus, of course, he couldn't offer to buy it for the amount he would sell it for. There were overheads; profits to be made; the car might sit there for months before he moved it. Tight-lipped she listened as all the positives he'd extolled about the car when she bought it were suddenly negatives. Finally she got him to agree to buying the car back for half the amount she'd paid and he'd throw in what he described as 'a good runner'. An hour later she arrived at work, courtesy of the secondhand car she now owned. And with a cheque for £8000 in her bag. She'd see Mum tonight and hand over that money – Terry Please had been asked to write it in Beth's name – and she'd tell her about the money in her bank account. And the rest that she was hoping to raise from selling possessions she no longer needed. They'd sit down together and work out an action plan. Negotiate with their creditors and work hard, together, to pay it all off. It might take them a couple of years but they could do it, she was confident they could. And once they had done that, why, they could do *anything*. Surely two like-minded, determined, women would be unstoppable once they joined forces.

Wishes

Naomi's gran had a saying she often used, 'Wishes won't wash dishes.' Mum always said that was wrong. It was meant to be something about horses. 'If wishes were horses...' So Gran said 'No way can a wish be a horse. That's just plain daft.' Still, they both agreed in principle that sitting around wishing things were different would help no-one. And yet, when it came to birthday cakes and blowing out candles, there they'd be, urging Naomi to 'Make a wish – but don't tell us what it is or it won't come true!' Very confusing. Adults just couldn't make up their minds.

When Naomi was old enough for High School she had a teacher who was for ever setting bizarre-seeming titles for English essays. For one of them, he read a quote from Aesop about the idea that having wishes granted would probably make us unhappy. He told the class to discuss this idea in their next homework essay. Naomi thought it was stupid. The whole idea of wishes was that you made your life better, so how could it be a bad thing? She wrote about the things she wished would happen in her life and in the world in general; she wrote about all the ways you could make a wish (on a star, especially a shooting one, or when a black cat crosses your path, or when you pass someone on the stairs, but only if you have your fingers crossed behind your back); she wrote about how life could be more fun if there were a way to grant wishes. It was the most she'd ever written for an essay and she was proud of her efforts. It came back with a D+ on the top and the comment, *'You have not attained the required depth for this essay and your response lacks maturity. You need to consider the realities of life.'* He wasn't Naomi's favourite teacher.

When she left school (at the earliest opportunity) she wanted to find a job that would be interesting and fun. She ended up working in a supermarket, stacking shelves. The only excitement coming from an occasional stint on the checkout. Funnily enough, the more she considered the realities of her life, she more she felt wishes were important. She certainly wished she could be somewhere else, doing something different. 'Which just goes to show how wrong teachers can be,' she thought, as she was bumped and jostled to and from work on the bus. Sitting there, pinned in her seat, with elbows and feet coming from all directions, her mind would wander off into pleasanter places where only good things happened. Wishing she were a famous dancer... or a desert explorer... or a great writer ... now that would be one in the eye for Mr D+. Definitely *not* wishing to be a shelf-stacker. Unfortunately, her daydreaming was so attractive that on several occasions she went right past her stop and ended up late for work. She was warned that one more late arrival would lose her the job.

'We value everyone here,' the manager said pompously (and, in Naomi's opinion, not at all truthfully), 'and we need each person to be here when they're meant to be. Otherwise it lets down all the others who come to work on time.'

She was given an official warning - so for a whole two weeks she tried desperately to stay alert and get off the bus at the right stop. A couple of times she managed to catch an earlier service just in case she slipped up, giving her time to get back to where she should have got off. But there was something so soporific about being on the bus that inevitably she messed up again. The job was gone. Now what would she do?

Confessing to Mum she'd lost the only job she'd been able to get so far was daunting. Seeing Mum's tightened expression, knowing her Mum would be wondering how they could make ends meet now, was upsetting. Hearing the resignation in Mum's voice was even worse.

'I suppose it's lucky you lasted this long,' she said, 'knowing what a dreamer you are.' Just for once it would be nice if Naomi could make her proud. Nicky round the corner had two teenage daughters. One working for a plumbing supply merchants, where she was already in charge of the Enquiries desk, and the other had just got on to a secretarial course. Now, if only *her* daughter could do as well for herself.

Naomi went to the Jobcentre first thing the next day but there didn't seem to be anything she could do. Nor anything she could train for. Mooching about the house was no good. Gran just kept muttering about idle hands doing the devil's work and it was too cold to sit around in the park for hours each day. She sighed. Just sixteen and she was on the scrapheap. Maybe she should have tried harder at school and stayed on.

Wandering around the town centre, ostensibly looking for 'cards in windows offering jobs', as per Mum's instructions, but really just wandering, she bumped into Molly. At one time they'd been good friends at school but as they got older the differences in their backgrounds became more obtrusive. There was a disastrous occasion when she'd invited Molly round 'for tea'. Her friend was clearly not much at ease and phoned as early as possible for her father to come and fetch her, using the excuse that she really should be home in time to exercise her pony. It was only when Naomi had a reciprocal invitation back that she glimpsed just how odd and poor her home life must have seemed. There was a proper dining-room with wood panelling all around and a big chandelier above the table. No beans on toast, squashed at the edge of a table in the kitchen or off a tray on your lap in front of the tv. A proper *meal.* The house was enormous, detached, surrounded by beautiful gardens. When Naomi commented on the amount of cleaning her friend's mum must have to do, there was a pause as Molly regarded her with disbelief, then announced,

'Mummy doesn't do cleaning. That's what we pay people for.'

There was something in her voice that suggested Naomi's mother too could pay people to clean for her if she just bothered to sort it out. Something that reckoned living in a grand house was all about making an effort, rather than being lucky who you were born to. Naomi felt she had been judged as not up to standard. Slowly the two of them had allowed the friendship to cool off.

But in contrast to Naomi's prejudices about wealthy people, Molly had actually grown into a nice person. When she heard about the job situation she insisted on buying Naomi a coffee. The two of them sat and chatted for ages about all sorts of things. Molly had so many plans for the future. Not wishes, or daydreams, but actual plans. Listening to her talk enthusiastically about the psychology course she wanted to do after A levels, and how she wanted to help people with problems, Naomi suddenly got a glimpse of a bigger life. It wasn't just about getting a job but about making a difference. She wished she had a big ambition like that. Before they left Molly promised to ask her father if there were any openings at his offices, and took Naomi's number so she could get in touch. Her mother was giving Molly a lift but it was in the wrong direction to take Naomi too so she said it was not a problem, the walk would do her good.

'It's miles,' said her old friend. 'Let me lend you the bus fare.' But when she checked in her purse she didn't have enough cash left after paying for the coffees. 'I know, you can use my bus pass. The photo's a bit blurry and anyway the two of us look pretty much alike. Remember how we used to make-believe we were twins?'

She thanked Molly, then, clutching the pass in guilty, sweaty hands, she ended up boarding a bus home. The driver hardly glanced as she proffered the card in its plastic wallet. Molly was right. It wasn't a problem.

Later that evening she got a call. It was a rather apologetic one.

'I'm really sorry, Naomi, but Daddy says there's nothing available at present. It's the financial situation. There may be an evening job, but it's just cleaning the offices. I can let you have a contact number for the cleaning company if you like...'

There was no point in false pride. Any job would be a good job. At least for now. She took the details gratefully and thanked Molly for her efforts.

'Oh, and thank you for the loan of the pass too,' she added in a lowered voice. What would Mum say if she overheard! 'Shall I post it back to you?'

'Oh, don't worry about it. I never use it anyway. Mummy and Daddy are always giving me lifts. I call them my private taxi firm! Just throw it away.' After wishing her good luck for the cleaning job she said goodbye and hung up. Naomi stared thoughtfully at the pass. Maybe she could hang on to it for a few days, while she was getting started at a job and earning again. Even with a wage coming in, by the time she'd paid a share of household expenses there wasn't going to be much left.

She phoned the cleaning company first thing in the morning and the man she spoke to agreed to give her a try. The hours weren't popular and he had trouble getting hold of reliable people. She would have to arrive at the offices after 6.30 that evening, when all the staff had gone, and he would show her what to do. There was a lot of talk about confidentiality – papers in bins to be disposed of without being read – and being able to organise herself. She would have two floors of the building to work around and it was up to her to manage all the work in the allotted time. If she managed well enough, more work and more hours would be offered to her. Did she think she was up to it? Naomi tried to sound enthusiastic and willing.

It was a long wait till the appointment so she finished a few jobs around the house, left her mum a note explaining where she was going, and then set off to catch the bus to town. Arriving early for once, she hung about outside the building before going in. Dave Shawcross seemed like a decent man to work for and he knew exactly the standard of work that could be achieved since he was used to covering when there were staff shortages. His little business was thriving, with contracts all over the town centre. He got out the equipment she would need, stayed with her to help her with the first of her floors, then took off, telling her he'd be back just before she was due to stop to check on the quality of work. She wasn't much of a fan of cleaning at home but somehow it seemed different doing it here. The offices were so quiet and calm. Everything was fairly orderly anyway, so just straightening up wasn't too bad. She dusted and hoovered, emptied bins, wiped down windowsills and door handles. She mopped toilet floors and cleaned around bowls and basins. As she finished each room she stopped and looked back, checking the first view the office staff would have in the morning. It was really satisfying, even though it was all the same tasks over and over again. And once she'd got into a sort of rhythm, she found her mind could drift away while her body worked on. Dave was pleased when he came along for his inspection and offered her the job for real. He explained that most nights he would be in and out, just checking that each person was doing what they should, but he gave her a mobile number to call in case of any problems.

Her mum was pacing up and down when Naomi got home and read her the riot act about taking on a job where she would have to travel home alone so late at night, but when it was pointed out that this was the only job likely to come along for a while she calmed down a bit. Then Naomi explained that she would only have to travel *to* the job by bus. Coming home, the company paid for minicabs – this being necessary if they were to recruit enough staff. Especially female staff. Almost all the employees currently on Dave's books were either mums, trying to earn a bit extra after the children were in bed, or students, paying their way through university.

So it was settled. After the first couple of weeks Dave offered longer hours and she accepted, working a six hour shift till after midnight. Of course, this meant that most mornings she wasn't out of bed till after Gran and Mum had gone for the day. Hours stretched before her with nothing much to do. Daytime tv was rubbish, she decided, and she began casting about for things to do. She dug out her old library card and started reading again – something she hadn't done for a long time. She took to walking round the local park, and once or twice a week made it to the swimming pool for a bit of exercise. She could only get to see friends on weekends, which was just as well. She was beginning to lose touch with them a bit. They had divided, quite unintentionally, into two groups. One for those who were still at school and planning to study more. They had little money but lots to talk about. Given half a chance they could change the whole world between them. The other for those who, like Naomi, had left school to start work. They were less into the talking and planning, more into the getting drunk and having fun. Some of them spent their entire week's earnings in one evening! Obviously their wage wasn't needed at home. Lots of them were pairing up and announcing engagements, though she suspected most wouldn't actually get far. Naomi couldn't decide whether she felt left out or left behind. It seemed she didn't have the ideas to fit in with the first lot, nor the money to hang around pubs all night with the second. It was very hard not to feel envious of everyone, and she did wish things had worked out differently for her, pleased though she was at having a job.

Having so much spare daytime on her hands she found herself using Molly's bus pass more and more. With unlimited free travel until it expired, it seemed a shame not to use it as fully as possible. She worked out a route around town, using five different buses, that gave her a tour of the entire centre, some of the bigger estates, and out into the country, yet still had her back in time for work. It took a whole afternoon so on her bus tour days she started packing up a little picnic – a sandwich, an apple, a bottle of drink – which she would have as her tea. If the weather were good enough she would sit on the grass near the bus shelter in one of the villages and eat it while she waited for her connection.

She loved to see the people getting on and off the different buses. Instead of being turned inward to her own dreamy thoughts, she found herself concentrating on the other passengers. Making up little stories in her head about where they were going and why. It was like an ever-changing soap. Since she always sat up the back of the bus, she called it 'Backenders' in her head.

'Hours of harmless fun, isn't it?' said a voice in her ear.

She turned, startled out of her latest episode, to see an elderly woman perched on the seat beside her. She must have been very absorbed not to notice the woman getting on.

'And you're right,' the woman said with a smile, 'it is just like a soap. Why there's humour, tragedy, sadness, laughter, all mixed-up in everyday events. Just like a soap. Just like life.'

Naomi felt a bit wobbly.

'Sorry...' she hesitated, 'was I saying things out loud?'

Ohmigod, if that was the case, she'd never dare get on a bus again for fear people would think she was nuts.

'Oooh no, you're not nuts, dearie. And you weren't saying things out loud.'

She smiled encouragingly at Naomi as if urging her to work something out.

'But you... but you're .... but this.... '

'Yes dearie. Somehow I know what you're thinking. Sorry about that but it kind of goes with the job.'

'Wh-what sort of job means you can read minds?' she stuttered out.

'Fairy Godmother.'

There was a pause. Naomi looked at her companion. Small, wrinkly, grey-haired, smiley. Potential for the FG post. But... a little red woolly hat and warm winter coat, thick stockings that even Gran would refuse to wear, stout lace-up shoes, and a shopping trolley. Well, really. There had to be a better explanation.

'You don't like my outfit?' the woman pouted.

Then almost imperceptibly, she started to change. There was a shimmering around her which gradually cleared away to reveal... an elderly, grey-haired lady in a tight fitting scarlet cropped top, bare navel sagging below, and low-slung skin-tight white capri pants. A bit of tummy folded gently over the top. Her bare, blue-veined legs ended in the most ridiculous pair of heeled sandals Naomi had ever seen. She felt sure even a model would have trouble walking in those.

'Stop it!' she hissed, looking round frantically in case anyone had noticed. 'Take them off!' And then, spotting a twinkle in the woman's eye, she added, 'And put the other stuff back on!'

'So you prefer my staid and sensible look?' she enquired, sitting there demurely, once again the very picture of respectability.

'Yes,' said Naomi, 'and I'm sorry if my thoughts about your outfit seemed a bit impolite. But I don't really have control over what pops into my mind.'

'Nobody does, dearie. Why the things I come across would make a girl like you blush crimson. There ought to be a Government Warning stamped across most people's foreheads.'

'So you actually can know what people are thinking, then? And you really are my Fairy Godmother, just like in the stories?'

'No, I'm afraid not,' came the reply. 'I'm not *your* Fairy Godmother. I am THE Fairy Godmother. There's only one. And I'm it.'

'And you're sitting on a bus,' said Naomi, feeling a little odd, 'just chatting to me and reading my mind.'

'Hmmm, perhaps we've stretched your credulity muscle a bit too much for one day. I'll call in and visit again soon.'

And with that she was gone. No pop as she disappeared. No gradual fading. One moment she was there and the next... nothing. Looking around, Naomi couldn't see any of the passengers looking perplexed or disturbed. It was as if the encounter had never happened.

'And maybe it didn't.' she thought.

All her life she'd been told she had a vivid imagination.

'Well, this is what happens to people with vivid imaginations. They definitely go nuts.'

The following morning the whole thing seemed even more bizarre and the best policy, she felt, was not thinking about it. 'Otherwise, it'll do my head in,' she told her reflection as she brushed her hair. Just to be on the safe side, she decided to avoid buses as much as possible for a few days. After lunch she headed to the park with a few slices of stale bread (for the ducks) and her latest acquisitions from the library (to improve her mind). A satisfactory plan to avoid total mental meltdown, she reflected, as she sat on a bench by the pond.

'So total mental meltdown is a possibility, then?' enquired a voice at her side.

Dropping bread and books everywhere, she swivelled round to see a young and undeniably gorgeous woman sharing the bench. She looked like one of those model girl cum lawyer types they had on American cop shows. Manicured nails, smart leather briefcase, a suit that screamed 'designer label'. If it hadn't been for the red woolly hat, that quite spoiled the ensemble, Naomi would never have guessed.

'Ooops! Forgot about the hat,' the woman smiled. She pulled it off and stuffed it into the briefcase. 'Habit,' she explained, 'I do tend to wear it a lot. So good for keeping the ears warm.'

Naomi gulped. 'It is you then?'

A nod.

'And you are real?'

Another nod. A pause. Then...

'You're wondering what I want with you?'

It was Naomi's turn to nod, so she did.

'I'll give you the condensed version. Try to keep up.'

She then began to speak extremely fast.

'Okay, long story short. Took the job on when the last fairy Godmother retired. Didn't think it would be a long-term job, just thought, you know, a bit of pin money... Anyway, had all sorts of daft ideas about it. People make wishes, I come along and grant them. Bish, bash, bosh, all done and dusted. Only it's not like that.

The whole wish thing goes dreadfully wrong. Soon found out. Well...' she paused for a quick breath, 'gave that up and decided to go at things a different way. So here I am.'

She beamed at Naomi.

'You gave that up?' Naomi asked slowly. 'You had the power to grant wishes and you gave that up?'

Another nod.

'You said the wish thing doesn't work. What do you mean?'

The woman gazed across the pond to where a young girl, about Naomi's age, was sitting on the grass, pulling up tufts and throwing them into the water. She looked desperately unhappy.

'The one thing that poor child wants, more than anything in the world, is to be beautiful.'

'But she is,' exclaimed a puzzled Naomi. 'I'd love to look as good as that.'

'Ah, but she doesn't know it,' said the Fairy Godmother. 'Now I could tweak a little magic her way, ratchet up the beauty factor by a few notches, and she'd have boys swooning all over her, even more than they do already. Only thing is, she still wouldn't see it. She'd think they were teasing or having a laugh at her expense. She'd never believe anyone who told her something she knows can't be true. Doesn't matter what I do on the beauty front, she'd never be happy.'

'Is there nothing you can do for her?' asked Naomi, feeling rather sorry for the girl.

'Already am,' came the smug reply. 'I'm working on her confidence and self-esteem. It's a long job, no immediate results, but we'll get there in the end.'

'And is that what happens with all wishes?'

'Too right. Give something too easily and people don't feel they deserve it, or they don't even recognise it. They either carry on just the same or get more miserable. No, granting wishes isn't all it's cracked up to be.'

'Then what do you do now?'

She puffed out her chest, beamed with delight, and announced proudly,

'Life Coach. Did a course in it and everything. I can show you my certificate if you like. Granted I only got top marks because I knew what the examiner wanted to read, but never mind, I picked up the gist of it.'

'Which is?'

The woman leaned closer and said,

'Wishes won't wash dishes.'

Naomi almost howled in frustration.

'You sound exactly like Mum and Gran! Just for once, couldn't somebody give me some advice that actually means something?'

'You really want advice?'

Yes!' said an exasperated Naomi.

'Then listen up, girlie, I'm about to start coaching.'

At first she asked about the things that Naomi liked doing. It was surprising how long a list it was, but even little things counted. Everything Naomi thought of was written down in a folder produced, with a flourish, from the briefcase. There was a line down the middle of the paper and the list almost filled the left-hand column. Then she asked about the things Naomi would like to achieve in her life. These were written down on the right-hand side. This too was quite a long list. Naomi was impressed that she'd actually got ideas. Then Fenella, as the Fairy Godmother had asked to be called, announced that was enough for one day or Naomi would be late for work and that would never do. She pulled another bag from her briefcase.

'Your tea, dearie. You can eat it on the bus. Take these notes with you, think about them, and I'll see you soon.'

And instantly she was gone as if she'd never been there.

Work went by in a dream that night, as she went over and over in her mind all the things on her list. She wasn't sure where it was leading but at least it felt like a positive move. Over the next few days Fenella popped up in all sorts of unlikely places: the library;

the street; Naomi's bedroom; even the next cubicle at the pool when Naomi was getting changed. She got Naomi to go over all the ideas she had ever had. They discussed some, discarded others, linked some together and, finally, came up with the definitive idea.

'So, said Naomi, 'what I really want to do is to be a screenwriter. But how likely is that? I quit school. I don't have many GCSEs, and the ones I do have aren't very useful. Not for screenwriting. It's all very well finding something I'd love to do but if I can't do it, what's the point?'

Fenella sighed. 'You give up too easily.'

She turned to a clean sheet of paper. Wrote 'HERE' at the bottom and 'THERE' at the top.

'Right then. This is you, here,' she tapped the paper, 'and this is where you want to be. All you have to do is figure out the steps to get you from HERE to THERE. And don't worry,' she said, catching sight of Naomi's bewildered expression, 'I'm going to help you.'

Together they trawled through all the resources at the library, both on the shelves and via the Internet. They costed things out. Worked out timings and, eventually, came up with The Plan.

'My life plan!' announced Naomi. 'And you know what? I've realised now that I might never get to 'there', but at least I'll have tried, and I definitely won't still be 'here'.'

'And so my work is done!' exclaimed Fenella in a very theatrical tone. The two of them giggled.

'I'll miss you being around,' said Naomi.

'Not for long, dearie, you're going to be too busy making your dreams come true. All those stories,' she tapped Naomi's head, 'it's about time they reached a wider audience.'

Naomi waited for the weekend before telling Mum and Gran she had something to talk over with them. When they were all sitting around the kitchen table she took a deep breath and started to explain all about her newly-found ambition. About the day classes on Creative Writing she could attend while still keeping on her evening job. How she could study part-time for a couple of A levels . She discussed the eventual possibility of a three-year Open University course. The availability of grants for people like her. The jobs she could do to fund her learning. She showed them a prospectus for a Film Study Centre in London.

'I know it all seems a bit much to take in,' she said, 'but I've had a lot of thinking to do lately. I don't want my life to just drift by, I want to make something of myself. Use whatever talents I've got. It'll take me years just to get started but I know where I'm going now.'

She was surprised by their reactions. Both Mum and Gran got a bit teary-eyed.

'I always knew you had it in you to do something special,' said Mum as they hugged.

Gran sniffed, then announced,

'And haven't I always said, wishes don't wash dishes. Get out there, Naomi, and show the world what you're made of!'

Argent

Once many years ago a child was born with eyes of silver. Do not be misled and think they must have been blue eyes with a silvery glint, or the palest of eyes that took on a hint of silver in certain lights. No, these eyes were a pure shining silver, like molten metal. By day they sparkled and reflected the light. By night they acquired the soft lambency of the moon and seemed to give forth a gentle glow.

The boy, for he was a male child, was born into humble circumstances. His parents worked their small strip of land just as their neighbours did. Just as previous generations had done. Alongside each small cottage a few chickens scratching about in the dust. A couple of goats. An occasional pig or donkey or milk-cow. Lines of carefully tended potatoes, cabbages, turnips. Green corn growing tall and turning gold under the summer sun. The lives of the people in that small community made a long intertwined story of hard work and shared problems. The troubles of a poor harvest or a river overreaching its banks or fierce storms that could smash a crop into the mud – these were endured by all. Good times were shared too, with much laughter and joy.

Just as there was a season for the lambs to appear in the spring, so each year's autumn and early winter brought most of the village's new babies. Nine months after the darkest and coldest months three, four, or sometimes more, new arrivals would bellow and wail their way into the world. Each one was a treasure to set aside against the future, a child who would one day be able to provide for their family.

The baby with the silver eyes was the firstborn to his parents. Newly birthed, he had been wrapped in a clean length of material, shown briefly to his father who hovered in the doorway, then handed to his exhausted mother. She held him close to her, examining his tiny features, his cross-looking face screwed up and reddened, eyes tight shut. His tiny mouth opened and closed like the gills of a fish just landed on the bank of a stream, trying to breathe in this new environment. Then his long, curled lashes fluttered apart and he opened his eyes. Unfocussed, they gazed her way briefly before his lids closed over them once again. She made a sound of alarm and distress. The village midwife and the husband hurried to her side, wondering what was amiss. 'His eyes!' she gasped. At first they did not know what she was talking about but as they urged her to explain, their voices roused the child. His head lolled around toward them and, again, for a moment or two his eyes opened. A flash of bright silver left them dumbfounded.

The midwife had helped birth all the village children since she was scarcely more than a child herself, learning from her mother who had in turn learned the skills from her mother. And so it went back through time. Never had she seen or heard of such a thing occurring. Fearfully they checked the small body again for other unusual signs or any marks that might signify the devil's influence. There were none. This baby was perfectly normal, save for his astonishing eyes.

By now neighbours were arriving at the rough-hewn wooden door to the cottage, bearing small gifts of welcome for the newest member of their community, expecting as was usual to be shown the child.

Instead they were turned back with a hasty excuse and the midwife slipped away to consult with her elderly mother. Of course, rumours began to spread. Perhaps the child had not survived. Such a thing was not uncommon. Perhaps it had been born with terrible deformities. A worse prospect even than death, since such a child could only ever be a burden on the community. Perhaps – and men nudged each other slyly at this one – perhaps, the young father had seen evidence that the child was not his. This too was not unknown.

When the midwife returned and the father opened the door, his face anxious, the small crowd gathered nearby awaiting developments saw her give a small shake of her head. Looking perplexed, the young man gazed beyond her. His eyes fell upon the faces of his friends and neighbours. Realising he must let them know, he gathered his thoughts, drew himself up straight, and invited them in. In groups of five or six they took turns to squeeze into the one-roomed home. Shyly the wife turned a well-wrapped bundle toward the first of them. They saw the baby's face and smiled and congratulated the couple. 'Wait,' said the father, 'and watch.' They stood for some time, puzzled but interested. The new mother sat her child up straighter and cooed and jiggled him until he opened his eyes. The silver eyes stared vacantly and unknowing toward them. The collective gasps and cries of astonishment reached the ears of those outside who began to clamour for their turn to come in. By now the whole community had gathered, eager for news. The first of the visitors stumbled outside into the full daylight, shaking their heads in a mystified way. When others asked what was going on, they were told, 'Wait and see, for you would never believe otherwise.'

It was one of the older women who said, on seeing the baby, 'This is a wondrous thing. Silver is the metal of wealth and good fortune. Surely this child will become someone of importance. He is a gift to all of us; a promise of better times.' She had lived for many years, so old that none still lived who had known her when she was young. Her opinion was treated with respect, her views given credence. And so it was that everyone agreed Argent, as the child was named, would one day do wonderful things and bring great prosperity to all.

As he grew his every achievement was noted and discussed. When he first showed awareness of his parents' presence; when he managed solid food; his first word. He was the measure by which others judged the progress of their own children – whose achievements were, alas, always too soon or not soon enough. There was no shortage of volunteers to watch over Argent and the child was never left to cry for more than a second or two. Someone was at his beck and call at every moment of the day.

By the time he grew older and began to take his first steps, he was already aware of his own specialness. People ran to him whenever he called out; were swift to comfort him; allowed him the best of everything. He was never scolded. He never had to deal with the rough and tumble activities of his peers. One glance from his beautiful silver eyes was enough to grant him his own way. As his understanding grew, he became aware that he had a special mission in life and because of this he was the most important person in the village. It was a very great power for a child to be granted and, as might be expected from a child, he abused the power given to him. He took pleasure in bullying other children. He would make them run errands for him. He would demand to be given a child's favourite toy only to break and discard it within minutes. As he grew older his behaviour grew more subtle. He would order the others to ostracise one child, or force two friends to fight each other. He particularly enjoyed telling them to do something which would bring the wrath of a parent and a sound beating. None of them would tell about his behaviour for fear of invoking the displeasure of the adults. They knew that no-one could speak against Argent.

His parents had continued to produce children at fairly regular intervals. Two boys and three girls followed him. All of them perfectly ordinary. It underlined even further how unusual he was. Argent's brothers and sisters were treated no differently than any of the other children in the village, except by Argent. Not only could he bully them outside the home but he lorded it over them inside. Their lives were made miserable by their older brother and none of them loved him. His doting parents could never see what was before their eyes – it seemed they were too bedazzled by his unusual beauty.

When he reached adolescence there was a marked sense of expectation. Surely now would be the time for his wonderful abilities to be revealed? Every action was scrutinised for clues as to what they would be. Yet … nothing changed. The other children were by now working the fields alongside their parents but not Argent. He was to be allowed to develop as nature or the gods intended. Without the disciplines of life he frittered his days away.

Other boys and girls were beginning to pair off and marry but there was no one for Argent. Those who had grown up alongside him had no love for him. And to Argent's parents, no girl in the village was good enough for him. They discussed the matter with the elders and came to the conclusion that a girl would have to be found from outside their community. Each family pushed itself to the brink of starvation in order to set aside sufficient crops to pay for a marriage bond and word was sent out about the amazing young man who would, one day, achieve greatness. Soon a young girl was found. She came from a wealthy family that owned a quantity of land some hours distant. Madreperl was brought by her parents to meet the young man with the silver eyes. Argent turned his gaze disdainfully upon her but she saw only the beauty this strangeness gave him. She fell in love with him and agreed readily to the proposed marriage. For his part, Argent cared less than nothing. As long as his needs were met, that would be all. And soon his great purpose would make itself known. Perhaps he would fly through the heavens like the gods. Perhaps the sound of his voice would bring death and destruction to any enemies. Perhaps a wave of his lordly hand would secure immense crops at the next harvest. He loved to wonder how his talent would reveal itself. And to imagine the villagers falling at his feet in admiration. He had begun to suspect that, when his children were born, they too would have the silver eyes that marked him as Chosen. He would beget a dynasty of superior beings. They would be the new gods of his people. And he would be revered as the Great Father.

It did not take long for Madreperl to understand that what she had read in Argent's appearance as shyness, diffidence, nobility was in fact just a coldness and a complete disregard for others. For a while her girlish love held out, and she believed that eventually her husband would come to love her in return. She tried to be the best wife she could but her efforts were met with scorn. It was clear that Argent regarded her as so far beneath him that she meant no more than the goats in their field. Love died. But she had been brought up to be a dutiful young woman so she continued to be a good wife, caring for a man who cared nothing for her. As summer came around again her sadness began to lift for she recognised the unmistakeable signs of pregnancy. Once Argent knew he showed more interest in her daily activities. Far from pleasing her, this new interest was an added burden for she understood he regarded her as he might a valuable brood animal. He went to great lengths to ensure she exercised, rested and ate at regular times. His doting parents saw this and believed him to have become a loving husband.

Finally the day came when Madreperl could no longer work on her vegetable patch but returned, pausing frequently to steady herself, to their cottage. She panted and groaned her way through her child's birthing while Argent sat watching from the corner of the room. He offered no words of comfort or encouragement. Indeed, it never occurred to him that he should. The midwife had arrived early for this most special occasion and could see it was going to be a long and difficult time for the young woman. The fire had burned down to embers, and Argent was slumped snoring in his chair, when the child finally struggled into the world. A tiny, delicate baby with skin of palest marble and wisps of silken hair. She, for Argent's child was a girl, fluttered long lashes as she took her first breaths and made the smallest of cries. Before the midwife could pass the child to her mother, Argent had awoken and snatched her up. He shook her rather more roughly than one would like, trying to rouse her to open her eyes. The midwife hovered nearby, anxious for the child. 'Look at me!' Argent demanded, in a loud and impatient voice. Amazingly the child responded and her lids parted to show eyes of the softest shade, a cloudless spring sky of blue, just like Madreperl's. Argent hissed angrily and cast the child aside, careless of whether her brains might be dashed out upon the floor or her tiny limbs broken and crushed. Madreperl screamed in horror but the watching midwife caught up the child and held her safe. Now Argent turned his attention upon his wife. 'Whore!' he snarled. Her eyes became huge and round, dark bruised circles of exhaustion beneath them. She looked at him stunned and uncomprehending. 'This is not my child! You think you can pass off another man's bastard as mine?' He flung the words at her then, turning towards the door, called over his shoulder, 'When I return, you and that mewling brat had better be gone. You are no wife of mine!'

The door slammed against the frame, the force of his anger reverberating through the small home. The midwife and the baby both began to sob but Madreperl dashed away the few tears that threatened. Now was not a time for weakness. She had a child to care for, even if the child's father rejected both of them. She sent the midwife ahead to tell Argent's parents what had happened. Once alone she began the painful task of dragging herself from the bed and pulling together the few items she could carry with her. Then, with her child snugly wrapped and held in the crook of one arm, she pulled her bundle towards her. She walked slowly out of the home into which she had poured so much love and care. She gave not a single backward glance, but straightened her back and made her way through the darkened, sleeping village. A light wavered dimly from the cottage of her in-laws and they came to greet her in the doorway, Argent's mother weeping with distress. For a while both grandparents took turns to hold the child they knew to be their blood. Then, sadly, passed her back to Madreperl. 'He is Argent's,' they agreed, 'we have no doubt of that. You have been the best of wives to him. Perhaps when he has got over his disappointment...'

But Madreperl shook her head. 'He will never accept our child,' she said, 'and I cannot let her grow up with a father who despises her.'

Her mother-in-law asked what she would do but there was only one possible course of action. She must return to her home village and hope her own people would show greater kindness than her husband had done. 'We cannot ask you to stay with us,' said her father-in-law, 'Argent has not behaved well in this matter but we would not go against our son. Perhaps it would be better for you to leave. It is a long and difficult journey though and you are tired from the baby's birth. How will you manage?'

There was no answer to that. Either they would make it or they would die on the journey. Her in-laws added to her baggage as much food as they thought she could carry then urged her to start right away as the sun was already beginning to lighten the sky to the east.

Meanwhile her husband had made his way to the cottage on the edge of the village where his mistress lived. It was not her choice to be with Argent but he had demanded her bed. Without a husband as protection, for she had been widowed young, she had been forced to accept his unwanted advances and now lived in dread of his fist pounding upon her door. On this night he was particularly insistent, even brutal, as he took his anger and frustration out on her. Coming to his senses again, he found himself sprawled across Neera's bed. She was huddled in the corner of the tiny room. She had pulled a thin shawl around her shoulders to cover the torn clothing and bruises beneath and silent tears trickled down her face. He felt irritated by this sight and resentment that Madreperl had put him in this situation. His anger flared again and he left at once for his own home. If Madreperl and the bastard child were still there.... But no, his cottage was silent and empty when he reached it. He searched around for any hint as to Madreperl's occupancy – the weavings she had hung at the window, the jars of food she had preserved and stored for the winter, a skirt awaiting mending and now left, abandoned, on the wooden chest. All were flung unceremoniously out of the door, in the direction of the midden. Satisfied that she was gone, he fell onto the bed and slept soundly until the sun was high in the sky and his empty belly roused him. With no-one there to prepare his food he took himself off to his parents' cottage. His mother cooked for him and fussed around him but something was different. She had always loved him fiercely and had seen only the best in him. Now the mists of love were clearing from her eyes and she began to see that they had raised a son who was selfish and domineering, who cared nothing for others. He was lazy and greedy. He never thanked her. He never showed any appreciation to anybody. He spoke rudely to his father, with none of the respect a good son would show. She managed to keep her face still and unresponsive in front of her son and husband but when she was alone she let her tears fall freely for the son she had thought she knew, and the grandchild she would never know.

Her husband too was beginning to feel very differently about his son. There was no doubt in his mind that Madreperl was the wronged party in all this. More wronged than she might guess, since he knew of his son's visits to the cottage at the edge of the village. Most of the men knew and had looked for a way to stop what was happening without offending Argent. Neera had been a good wife to her husband before he fell ill and an even better one when he succumbed to the wasting disease that eventually killed him, nursing him through terrible months without complaint. And at his death she had clearly been heartbroken. Since when she had kept to herself. Until Argent started on her. His behaviour could not be condoned but how could anyone approach him about this? The problem had been eating away at the old man. He started to look at his first-born son through new eyes, and what he saw shamed him.

A strange sensation began to gnaw at Argent over the next few days. People still did everything he wanted or needed. The women had set up a rota for cooking his meals and washing his clothes, while he lived alone in bachelor splendour. The men spoke to him civilly when they passed by, and when he mentioned some damage to the thatch of his cottage it was repaired without delay. But something was missing. It wasn't respect or consideration. Just .... something he couldn't quite put his finger on. It was as if they were all in silent communication around him and he couldn't understand. To make matters worse he could no longer seek consolation with his mistress - at a moment's notice Neera had been removed from her cottage. The other women told her she had mourned long enough and she had been invited into one of their homes to join another family. She accepted with such alacrity that the men of the village knew for certain she had never wanted Argent's attentions.

The relief of being free of him brought back the smile to her face and gave a lightness to her step. Over the next few months the happy person she had been before her husband's illness returned. Before long, one of the single men had offered himself as a new husband. A proposal she was glad to accept.

So now that Argent couldn't avail himself of her he cast furtive glances around the other young women. All were married, spoken for, or watched with great care by their girlfriends and menfolk. Argent felt uneasy at the way the men 'assisted' the women whenever they were near him. He wondered if anyone had been aware of his visits to Neera. For a moment he felt a hint of shame. The very thing he had accused Madreperl of doing was, after all, his own sin. But he shrugged it aside and told himself they would all come flocking to *give* him their sisters and daughters, once his special nature finally revealed itself..

As time passed he became more and more isolated. He had never had friends and there was no closeness with his siblings but now the men made every excuse not to remain in his company more than was strictly necessary. Once or twice meetings were held by the elders of the village and nobody remembered to invite him along. It seemed his opinion was no longer to be sought. He was still treated with deference by other villagers. His needs were always provided for. But when people looked at him, there was no hint of admiration in their eyes. Finally the older inhabitants were realising the mistakes they had made. They suspected that their expectations of Argent's specialness had been in vain and would never be fulfilled now, but they had made him dependent upon them all. More from pity and the knowledge of their own foolishness, they continued to care for the strange young man who had such beauty in his eyes but such ugliness in his heart.

Years passed. Argent's parents were no longer living. His generation had become the elders of the village, among them his own brothers and sisters. None held any affection for him, only a sense of continuing duty inherited from their parents and grandparents. Over time the centre of the village had shifted. More and more homes had been built to the side furthest from Argent's cottage and, wanting more congenial neighbours that he, no-one had chosen to move into the homes surrounding his as they each grew empty. Older neighbours died and were not replaced. Their unused cottages soon fell into disrepair. Timbers, roof slates and floor slabs were plundered to use again on newer buildings. Slowly the forest reclaimed plots of land. And, without it ever being intended, Argent was living alone in his little cottage, just inside the forest boundary.

As children were born and grew, they knew him only as a hermit figure, a man with peculiar eyes and an unpredictable temper. Since their parents never chose to talk about him they were ignorant of his true story. He was an adult and yet he needed looking after. Like children everywhere they made up their own stories, mostly telling how his mind did not work properly or how he had grown mad, for they were the only explanations they could come up with. These stories were told and retold by generations of village children - partly for the fun of scaring themselves and partly to impress younger children. Sometimes for a dare one would be sent into the forest to spy on Argent from behind the bushes. They would often report back that he was pacing up and down the forest paths, muttering to himself. These mutterings the children repeated, trying to copy the man's gruff voice.

'My powers!' they would growl at one another, 'My powers must come soon. This waiting is unbearable.'

They would raise their heads to the darkening sky and howl in unison,

'Oooo-oh! Where are my special powers?'

Then, as one, they would burst into laughter and turn their attention to a game of catch, or would take turns throwing a rope ring around a target.

One day some of the younger girls were playing a pat-a-cake game to the rhythm of a song:

Eyes of silver, heart of stone,

In the forest, all alone

Eyes of silver, waiting yet,

You will …..

They sang so lustily that it took a while for the sound of slow hoofbeats to reach them all, and the song died away gradually. When they stopped they stared in amazement at the three people who had ridden horses into the village. The visitors seemed very grand and important. There was a good clear space at the heart of the village these days, with a patch of grass, and a pond for the ducks and geese. A wooden bench to one side gave a resting place for some of the older men, who loved to doze or gossip there on fine days. The horses had been ridden gently into this place and stopped. Two of the riders were guards, well-armed with sword and club. The third rider was a woman of great beauty. Long blonde hair spilled out from the hood of her cloak and soft blues eyes scrutinised the girls. She swung herself down from the saddle and smiled at them.

'You sang that song so well,' she told them, 'but it's one I've never heard before. Eyes of silver? What does that mean?'

And the children started to tell her all about the strange old man who lived in the forest and talked to himself. As they interrupted one another and vied to gain the attention of the beautiful lady, one of the older men heaved himself up from the bench and came over. He greeted the woman with a polite bow of his head and gave his name as Durand.

'You are asking about my brother?' he enquired politely, shooing the girls away with a wave of his hand and a stern look.

'Your brother?' She looked startled. 'The man with silver eyes does exist, then?'

'Indeed he does. Would that he had been born with the ordinary looks of the rest of his family.' He sighed. 'It is a sad story my lady and one that does this village no credit.'

'I am sorry to cause you pain,' she said softly, 'but I have good reason to wish to know whatever you can tell me.'

Durand looked at her for a moment then gestured to her to follow him to the bench and the shade of the tree under which it stood. Handing the reins to one of her companions she gave a few terse orders then turned and followed Durand.

He told her the story of the amazing birth of Argent and of how the villagers, in their ignorance and superstition, had placed such value on the child. How they waited year in and year out for some return on their devotion. And how such adulation and fawning had corrupted the heart and soul of a child so that he grew ever more full of himself and ever more monstrous. He told of a childhood blighted by the meanness of his older brother, and of his parents, who died with sorrow in their hearts at the way their firstborn had turned out. He told of Argent's increasing isolation and the madness that seemed to grow in him, as the special talents he believed would be his never arrived. As he finished his account she sat thoughtfully, considering all he had said.

'So this child was never special in any respect but the extraordinary colour of his eyes?'

Durand nodded.

'Such a wasted life.' he said. 'If only they had let him grow as all the other children did. '

'And is he the only one to be born like this?'

Another nod. 'Of all his brothers and sisters, nieces and nephews, none has been born like Argent. Why, even his own child....'

'He has a child?'

Durand sighed, 'Lost to us for many years, along with my sister-in-law. The child didn't even have a name when they left but she did have the bluest of eyes, according to my mother who held her but a brief time. So, no, thank goodness, no child born like him.'

Then she asked Durand if there might be a chance of seeing Argent for herself. He was reluctant at first but her interest seemed to stem from a genuine desire to learn and not from morbid curiosity. At last he agreed to take her to the cottage in the forest, as long as she kept her distance from his unpredictable brother and could bear to hear the foulness of his speech.

It took several blows of Durand's fist upon the door to rouse Argent. The figure that opened it and shambled outside was not an encouraging sight. Even from several feet away it was clear he reeked. His clothes were stained and hung loose upon a painfully thin figure. Uncombed hair and a straggling beard covered much of his face and his head was cast down, as he mumbled to himself.

'Argent, it is Durand, your brother, and see.... I have brought a lady visitor to you. Will you not greet her nicely?'

After a moment or two the mumbling stopped and Argent raised his head toward them. She gasped and stepped back, looking stunned. The eyes that looked her way were of the purest silver imaginable. They seemed to flow like liquid metal. Reflected in them she could see her own image staring back at her. Argent drew himself upright and smirked at her expression. Something of his old arrogant self rekindled inside.

'As you can see,' he quavered, 'I am no ordinary mortal. Well might you look in amazement. I am unique. I am a gift of the gods!'

'And what has your uniqueness given you?' she asked gently, 'Apart from your beautiful eyes?'

Anger flashed across his once-handsome face. 'You mock me!' he screamed at her. 'You mock me! And for that you will be punished. Punished! You hear me?'

He was getting louder and more incoherent with every word. Spittle frothed at the corners of his mouth.

'When my powers come, you will be sorry for your mockery. You will bow down and worship me, you will beg my forgiveness.'

He began to curse at her and scream more threats. By now Durand had a hand clamped tight around his brother's arm and was pulling him back towards the door with quiet rebukes and firm insistence.

'Now then, Argent, the lady meant no harm. There's no call for rudeness. You must calm yourself. Go back in and Murrin will fetch supper along shortly.'

Shouts and swearing and threats continued to issue from the cottage even after Durand had shut the door and started to guide the visitor back along the path. As they walked Durand apologised for his brother's behaviour. He felt that the woman wanted to say something in return but couldn't. Twice she made as if to speak, then thought better of it. So to make polite conversation he asked if she had ridden far that day.

'A few miles,' she offered, 'I had heard stories and I wanted to see for myself...' Her voice tailed away. 'I have children,' she said then. 'Two boys. I hope they have a happier life than that poor misguided soul we saw back there.' She shuddered. 'Yes,' she continued, 'my sons are just ordinary children, and I wish for them the most ordinary of lives.'

In return Durand told her of his own fine children and the families they were raising and so, in companionable mood, they reached the village centre. The woman thanked him for his time then, with the assistance of one of her guards, climbed back on her horse. She waved to the little girls, at their games once more, and headed back in the direction from which she had first appeared. As she rode a smile hovered about her lips as she thought of her darling babies. They were twins, just a few months old, and the image of their mother. So their doting father claimed. Yes, the image of their mother - apart from the eyes, of course. Theirs were pure silver, like liquid metal. But according to their great-grandmother, Madreperl, that was nothing to worry about, just a family trait. And now Argent's granddaughter knew the truth for herself and would make sure that silver eyes would be no more special than a dimple in the cheek or a curl to the hair.

Lessons

When Sylvia Rose retired there was a cake, a photographer from the local paper, and a rather dull speech from a representative of the Local Authority. A man who seemed to know little about schools and even less about Sylvia Rose. The school had got together a number of old pupils – quite literally 'old' pupils. Sylvia was shocked to see how grubby-kneed boys and giggly girls had turned into adults, parents, even grandparents. They all seemed to recognise her although she struggled to dredge individual pupils from her memory. Sometimes a name would be familiar. Sometimes a face. But most of them were strangers. The whole event had been planned with some care by her colleagues and she was appreciative of that, although her gratitude was tinged with the knowledge that most of them would heave a sigh of relief at her going. She wasn't the sort of person to change with the past and had been an immoveable block in the way of most people. It wasn't as though she still had the respect of pupils and parents. Children today were used to so much more stimulation and support. Sylvia blamed this on the fact that they spent all their time glued to the tv or fiddling with electronic gadgets whose workings were a complete mystery to her, and continued to teach as she had always done. And so it seemed her lessons did nothing to grab their attention or engage their interest, based as they were on the curriculum she had successfully used some forty-five years before. Parents used to be grateful that there was discipline and order in Miss Rose's class. That from year to year nothing changed. Nowadays they muttered about how strict she was, how the children complained of being bored. Few of them took issue with her directly. Too many of them had been in her class themselves. But headteacher after headteacher had tried to deal with their increasing dissatisfaction. There had been courses offered, some of which Sylvia even attended. She nodded along with whatever was said but kept to her own ways of doing things. There had been in-class support given. Another member of staff would work alongside her, desperately trying to introduce changes. But Sylvia continued to do things her way. The current headteacher had relied on the fact that Miss Rose would leave at sixty. Just a few months to go! The months went but Sylvia didn't. She had hung on, with the support of her union, until it was no longer possible to insist on staying in her post. Now, finally, she had to stop. Retire. So, surrounded by cards, gifts, balloons and banners, Sylvia thanked people politely, tried very hard to remember who they were, said all the right things … but inside she was terrified. She wanted to beg people to let her stay. Plead with them to be allowed to continue as she was. Because the job she did was all she was. Sylvia Rose only existed within her classroom.

When baby Sylvia was born the Second World War was drawing to a close. Her mother was in despair at her arrival. With her husband away for more than two years she had succumbed to temptation and got involved with a Scottish soldier stationed nearby. It wasn't that she had fallen out of love with her husband but a few letters exchanged at irregular intervals were no substitute for reality. She was lonely, struggling to manage both her work at the munitions factory and to keep a roof over her head and food on the table. When she met Donald he was so outgoing and cheery that it took her mind off everything else. At first she was able to convince herself they were just friends, enjoying each other's company. After all, she knew he was engaged to a girl back in Dundee and he knew she was waiting for Bob to return. But eventually they had started an affair. It only lasted a few weeks before Donald's unit was moved on. He reckoned it would be the final push and then life could get back to normal. He was right about the war ending but Sylvia's mother never felt life ever became normal again.

When she realised she was pregnant she was terrified. Two or three months gone, by her reckoning, and already showing quite noticeably in spite of the layers of loose clothing she had taken to wearing. After seeing a doctor she got transferred to lighter work in a nearby town and changed her digs. Her own family was scattered and they were only in touch by letter or phone. Nobody here knew her so it was easy to pretend the baby was her husband's, conceived when he had an unexpected leave. By now it was far too late to consider any option other than going through with the pregnancy, even if she had known who or where to ask for help. In desperation she clung to the idea that, if she had the child and gave it up for adoption straight away, her husband would never know and she could pretend it had never happened. Then the telegram came, informing her that Bob had been wounded in action. He was being shipped home to convalesce and would not be returning to his unit. There was no way she could keep him in the dark. As soon as he saw her their marriage would be over. It was unthinkable that she should be on her own bringing up an illegitimate child. She wrote Bob a letter confessing and begging his forgiveness. She assured him the child would be adopted, he would never have to see or hear of it again, and she pleaded for a second chance.

Bob hadn't exactly led a blameless life himself. There had been a few encounters with women. Paid encounters too. After all he'd been away from home comforts for a long time. However he came of a generation that could overlook such behaviour in men – not in women. He was furious when he read his wife's letter and ready to walk away from the marriage. As soon as he could walk, of course. But lying there day after day, trying to cope with the pain and the rehabilitation exercises, watching the support other men received from their wives and girlfriends, he began to change his mind. With the child gone they could start a family of their own. At least now he knew she was capable of having children. Although he'd have to keep her on a tight rein. Make sure there were no more incidents. She had always been a pretty girl. No wonder someone else had latched on to her. Well, he'd make sure she stayed home and behaved herself from now on.

When he eventually agreed to see her, Sylvia's mother was so relieved. She dressed as carefully as she could to minimise the look of the bump and carried a bag full of home-cooked treats for Bob which she was able to place strategically on her lap while they talked. It was a very strained conversation. After so long apart they were like strangers and the unseen presence of the baby made any talk of the future seem like a minefield. They were both careful with their words and alluded to the child as 'it'. Slowly they worked out a plan of action. Bob would come back to the digs she was living in as soon as he was fit enough to leave hospital. They would wait till it arrived, give it up for adoption, then move to be nearer to their own families. There they would make a fresh start.

But it wasn't to be. Sylvia's mother went into labour two or three weeks earlier than expected. It was a long and difficult labour. The doctor warned Bob his wife might not make it and suddenly he was gripped with fear. The feelings that had been suppressed for so long re-emerged and he knew he didn't want to lose her. In the face of this prospect her affair seemed unimportant, something they should be able to get past. He prayed that she might live and promised whoever was listening that he would forgive her affair and be a good husband, no matter what. And so Sylvia was born in the early hours of a chilly April morning just days before the bells would ring out to celebrate Victory in Europe. She was undersized and weak but at least she was alive. Unlike the twin who was born several minutes later. There was no time to hand her to her mother who was, in any case, barely conscious. She was whisked away for emergency surgery and her child was taken to the special baby-care unit. The nurses weren't surprised at Bob's lack of concern about the child when he took not the slightest interest in what would happen to her. Men were not expected to show their feelings publicly or have much to do with new-borns. His attention was focussed entirely on the wellbeing of his wife. For the next two days he paced the hospital corridors or sat smoking cigarette after cigarette in the waiting-room.

Slowly his wife recovered. Then came the moment when the doctor sat down at the bedside to explain matters to them. The birth of the first child had caused a problem that resulted in lack of oxygen reaching the second baby and in the haemorrhaging that had nearly cost her mother's life too. It would take time to recover from the operation but the damage was such that she would have no more children.

'Try to look on the bright side,' the doctor said gently, 'at least you have one healthy child. So many people never have that much.'

A few moments later, perhaps at the doctor's prompting, Sylvia was brought in to her mother. As she took her in her arms she knew there could never be an adoption. This was her child and she would not give her up, not even for marriage and respectability. Somehow she would have to face the world. She watched as tiny fingers curled around hers and tears began to fall as she thought of the second child she had lost and would never be able to hold. Bob stood paralysed, his dreams of a future with a dutiful wife and a son of his own fading. He had wanted his wife to live but there was a price to pay for it. Then somehow he found the words.

'All right, love, we'll keep her. I'll bring her up as my own. Turn off the waterworks now, there's my girl. We'll manage. We'll get through.'

They called her Sylvia. Bob hadn't wanted to use a name from his family. It would have felt wrong. His wife chose the name and he didn't question it. It was actually the name of a character in a film she had seen with Donald. The two lovers in the film were doomed to lose each other just as in their relationship. Of course she would never tell Bob about that and over the years when the film was occasionally scheduled for tv viewing she made a point of not watching it, feeling that it would be a betrayal of her husband. But the name brought back memories of a time she wanted to remember, to hold close. Just as she wanted to hold her child close.

To her Sylvia was so precious. An only child who could never be replaced. When she thought of all the months she had plotted to give her up for adoption it made her blood run cold. She coddled her child at every opportunity. Bob watched this with increasing irritation. The son he had dreamed of would never be, but in addition to being saddled with another man's child he was stuck with a girl. He made up his mind that she should grow up to be strong and capable. At least she would get that much from him. And she wasn't going to turn out right if he let her mother baby her all her life.

So throughout Sylvia's early years there was a very confusing clash of priorities operating around her. Her father had strict rules about how the house should be and how both she, and her mother, should behave. She was swiftly punished for any infringement and learned to be still and quiet whenever he was home from work. She was taught not to cry or make a fuss. Stiff upper lip was the order of the day. If she fell over and grazed her knee, there was no cuddling or soothing as antiseptic and plaster were applied. If she woke screaming from a nightmare there was no chance of her being lifted into her parents' bed and comforted, or a warm drink and a cuddle. 'It's just a dream. Go back to sleep.'

As she grew she was expected to help out around the house, doing chores before school and at weekends. And always as she worked at shining the family's shoes or fetching in a bucket of coal or washing the dishes, she hoped her father might give a word of praise for her efforts. The most that ever came her way was a grunt of approval. Playing out was not permitted though occasionally a neighbour's child would be allowed into the back garden to play with her. Most of the neighbourhood's youngsters ran free through the nearby fields and woodlands, or in the local park. On a warm summer's evening she could hear their shouts and laughter as she sat at the table and ploughed through her books. Her father had made up his mind that she should find a 'good' job when she was older and he was determined that she should be as successful in her studies as he could make her. 'A woman's place is in the home,' he taught her, 'looking after her husband. But until that day she shouldn't be messing about with fripperies or chasing after the lads. She should make a contribution to society.' It was a very bewildering mix of discipline and expectation

Her mother's priorities were very different. They revolved around her need to protect her child and keep her close at all times. When Sylvia was very small this was her source of comfort. Stolen cuddles and nursery rhymes when her father was at work. And the stories her mother made up for her. These were about the adventures of two little girls, Sylvia and Laura. For a while she was convinced she really did have a friend called Laura who played and laughed with her. But as she grew older her father's influence became greater. Every girl wants her father's love and acceptance. She became his shadow, helping with jobs around the house and garden. Even, occasionally, being allowed into his shed. A mysterious place with strange greasy smells and sharp tools everywhere that were never to be touched. Not because he was worried about her hurting herself. No, do that once and she'd soon learn not to do it again. Bob's concern was for his tools and the possibility that she might damage them.

She took on so many of Bob's ways and teachings that no-one could ever have taken her for anyone but his child. And her father certainly loved her, even if those years spent fighting had changed him for ever and made him into a man who ran his whole life along army lines and with army discipline. Routine, order, obedience. That's what he understood. They had brought him home alive when other men hadn't made it but they didn't make it easy for him to express his love for either his wife or the child he had come to think of as truly his own creation. Sylvia never knew Bob was not her biological father. He had agreed to put his name on the birth certificate and no-one ever questioned it or realised that at the time of Sylvia's conception her father was fighting for his life in Italy. It was certainly not something either of her parents ever wanted to refer to, even between themselves.

The isolation and strangeness of her childhood also remained unknown to Sylvia. She had no concept of how other families lived. When she was ready to leave school it never occurred to her that she should have any say in her future. That was up to her father. He attended a meeting with the careers teacher and Sylvia during which her opinion was not sought. Not that she had an opinion to offer. After considering her abilities they agreed that primary school teaching would be a good path to take and, as her father explained, would be very helpful when she married and had children of her own to care for. All that training would not be wasted when she became a full-time wife and mother.

When the choice of training college was being made Sylvia's mother put her foot down for the first and only time in her entire married life.

No way was Sylvia going away to college, even if she came home every weekend. There was a college two bus rides away, an all-girls college or her father would never have permitted it, and it was decided that she should attend college there but continue to live at home. It was just like going to school really, she thought, except that she had further to travel. Her commuting meant that she didn't get involved in any form of student life. She just attended the lectures, handed in assignments on time, and progressed fairly invisibly through three years of training. Around her the sixties were in full swing. Words to do with freedom and choice were everywhere but Sylvia's ears were closed to them. She dressed like a much older woman. All her clothes were chosen, or even made, by her mother. She liked making outfits for the two of them. Preferably matching, or in complementary colours. Sylvia's only pastimes were those shared with her parents. All choices and decisions were made by her father. All of her needs attended to by her mother. And so the pattern of her life was set. After passing her college courses with very high grades, she found a post at a local school. And there she had stayed. Marriage and children had never happened. She had set up routines and rules within her classroom, just as she had learned at home. These were not adjusted for anyone. Children had to conform, just as Sylvia had done. After all, she had done well for herself, hadn't she? And she was happy, wasn't she?

Losing her parents – first, her father and then, after a few years of decline, her mother – had been a terrible blow. She continued to live in their little terraced house, keeping everything as well-maintained and clean as her father and mother had done. It was a lonely life but she had her work to occupy her. Even holidays weren't so bad since she knew they would eventually be over and she would return. But now.... now there would be no return. And Sylvia was so afraid.

At first she tried to pretend it was just another school holiday. But as weeks drifted into months she felt she would go crazy if she stayed home any longer. She made a visit to her old school and volunteered her services as an unpaid classroom assistant. But her offer was politely declined as the headteacher explained that it could make for very difficult dynamics within the class and that she would find it very hard to switch off from being in charge. The children could be confused. She suggested trying a school slightly further away. Sylvia thanked her politely and walked outside, noticing that already there had been changes in the school. Things had been moved around; there was a new noticeboard; the wall displays had been replaced. There were hanging baskets outside the entrance doors. It didn't look the same. Bereft she walked all the way home. She could have caught the bus, but this used up a little time. And that's it, she thought, it's all about using up time. Is this all my life is about now? Do I just have to use up time until I die?

Had she been a person for attending the doctor's surgery, someone might have noticed as she slipped further and further into a depressed state. But she had always been taught not to bother doctors unless you had a visible injury that couldn't be dealt with by antiseptic and bandages. 'Don't make a fuss over nothing'. So her inability to sleep and the headaches she was suffering were ignored. And any opportunity to spot her mental and emotional deterioration was lost. In fact, had she gone to the local surgery they would have had difficulty tracking her paperwork as it had been so long since she had needed to see anyone. No visitors came to the house and her family had never been churchgoers. The postman was the only one who noticed any difference. Sylvia had not cancelled her subscription to a teaching magazine. It was too large to push through the letter-box without rolling it up and Sylvia's father had long since made it clear to the post-office that no item should be delivered folded, rolled, or in any way damaged. A rule that was still being followed long after he had gone. So every three months there would be a knock on the door and the postman would hand the pristine magazine to Sylvia.

When she had been working she had opened the door already dressed smartly, if somewhat frumpily, ready to go to work, and had taken it with a brisk 'thank you'. Over the course of the next year or two there was a marked deterioration until, one day, the rattle of the door-knocker resulted in the sound of slow, shuffling footsteps along the hallway. The previously pristine net curtains and the frosted door panel were yellowed and dirty looking. The paintwork beginning to look shabby. The postman stood taking this in as he waited. A sound of a key rattling in the lock, then the door inching open. A face peered vacantly around the edge. Hair straggled untidily down to Sylvia's shoulders. The postman had been covering this route for several years and knew quite a few elderly people who lived alone. He tried to keep an eye on them and let Social Services know of any problem. He was shocked at the sight of Miss Rose, though. She wasn't even elderly but she looked a good twenty years older than she should. And, as he became aware of a smell, he realised she wasn't looking after herself any more than she was her home. He tried to chat pleasantly to her as he handed over the post but it was as if she didn't even hear. She croaked a 'thank you' and closed the door again leaving him standing on the doorstep looking distinctly worried.

He phoned Social Services even before he had finished his round and over the next few weeks they made repeated efforts to speak with Sylvia. She either shut the door on them or shouted from inside to go away and leave her alone. Then came a day when they knocked and knocked but heard nothing. Concerned, the two women tried peeping through the windows. They even got round to the back garden – now an overgrown wilderness of nettles and bindweed - and tried the windows there. That was when they saw her, slumped in a chair, leaning on the kitchen table. A call to the police, and they were able to gain access. Sylvia was alive – but barely. 'Advanced pneumonia' was the diagnosis when she was taken to hospital. She was cared for in the ICU for just over a week but never regained consciousness before slipping quietly away. Still in her sixties and previously in very good health, she had become an unkempt, unwashed, malnourished shadow of herself in a matter of months. The local newspaper printed a story about how sad it was that a woman who had worked all her life only managed a year or two of retirement. They had a follow-up article on the inside page on the importance of planning for your retirement, with interests, hobbies, and networks of friends and family. For a week or two the letters page received various comments on the theme of people living alone and the lack of neighbourliness in modern society. Then life moved on.

And life moved on for Sylvia too. There was a long, confusing time, of recovery. She knew she was being cared for but found it hard to work out who, where, why. Remembering was difficult and somehow her senses didn't work the way they should. Her vision and hearing seemed to be gradually adjusting to strange new frequencies. She could see shapes and colours, hear sound, but couldn't process them or put names to them. She felt warm and comfortable. Safe. Even cherished. And so her mind veered away from trying to explain it all. She just knew she felt better than she had in a very long time.

The she became aware of a Presence. A Shining Presence, she thought. From it there emanated such a feeling of warmth, understanding, love. It spoke to Sylvia but not in words that could be written. And Sylvia understood that her old life was gone. She was somewhere that, in her own mind, she thought of as 'heaven'. She also understood that, when the time was right, she would move on from this place too. And, yes, one day she would be with her parents again. Meanwhile, what did she want to do?

Now that was a difficult question. The only thing Sylvia knew to do was being a teacher. She felt the Presence smile at her. Then suddenly they were elsewhere. And there were children. All ages, races, sizes. Some ran around laughing and chasing. Some sat, bewildered, sucking thumbs or hiding faces. Some looked so sad Sylvia felt her heart might break. The Presence explained to Sylvia that when children move on as she had done, they need time to adjust, to learn, and there was always a place for teachers. Some of the children had been very traumatised by their experiences and it would take a long time before they were able to leave this place. Others would be much quicker. But all needed love, understanding, and kindness.

'Then there are schools here?' asked Sylvia, fixed on the idea of them learning.

The Presence smiled again and words came into Sylvia's mind.

'Here there is anything you can think of.'

And the Presence was gone.

Sylvia looked around at the mob of children. Some barely more than babies. Others who looked as if they might be ready for Big School soon. Where could she possibly teach them? There was just a sensation of Nothingness around, a wispy almost-cloud feel. She thought with longing of her old classroom, set up just as she liked it. Instantly there it was. Everything solid and real. Even down to the scratched name of Anthony Williams on the side of her desk. Oh, she had been so angry about that! Her pens sat ready in their holder. Her notes were on the desk. It was perfect. She called to the children to come and sit at the tables. Most of them did so. Then she scooped up the others one by one. They sat for a few moments while she thought what to do. 'Right,' she announced in a clear voice. 'We'll start with the alphabet.' She turned to the board and began to write, noticing that instead of having the whiteboard and pens she'd hated so much, they had reverted to her beloved blackboard and chalk. Behind her she heard movement and swung around to tell the children to sit quietly. But they were no longer there. The room was empty. Save for one solemn-faced little girl.

She looked somehow familiar. Dark brown curls bounced around her head as she half walked, half skipped over to Sylvia. Removing the stick of chalk from Sylvia's grasp she regarded her teacher for a moment then shook her head. With a wave of her hand the room melted away. Without the walls blocking her sight, there were all the children sitting or playing in Nothingness, just as they had been when she first saw them. Then the little girl lifted Sylvia's hand and with it drew the shape of a letter A in the air. The letter became almost solid. The children looked around and many of them smiled or laughed and ran towards Sylvia. The shape floated and wobbled in the air, changing colour with dizzying speed. 'It's A,' she said to them, 'A for....ant.' As she said it an enormous bubble ant appeared. The children shrieked with delight and climbed on its back to ride. Or raced underneath its body. Sylvia was amazed and beginning to smile too, as she went through all the A s she could think of. 'Aardvark!' 'Apples!' 'Aeroplane!' With each suggestion, there it was until most of them were racing about shrieking and having fun. Even the shyer children came to hold Sylvia's hand and laughed aloud. They were having such fun that at first Sylvia didn't notice the Presence appear and stand watching them, smiling. When she did she understood that was enough for now. And found herself back in a room that she thought she recognised. There was a meal on the table and a comfortable bed. Sylvia knew this would be her home for a while. As she thought of home, objects she had known and treasured began to appear in the room and the room itself changed shape and proportion to fit everything in. There was the kitchen table and chair. Father's bookcase with his copies of Dickens and Reader's Digest. Her mother's sewing basket. The two china dogs that sat on the mantlepiece. She looked around and sighed with contentment.

There was no way to measure time in this strange new world. Somehow Sylvia would just know it was the right moment for lessons and then there she would be, surrounded by children. When she felt it was time to stop, back she would be in her own special home. And the lessons were not as she had thought they should be. She very soon realised that if the children didn't want to be in her world they could choose not to be there. And there was nothing she could do about it. If she wanted the children to learn anything it had to be fun. Then they would happily join her. She had also learned that teaching was fun for her too, when she could create an entire world with just a thought. The day she taught them about springtime, she created the most perfect woodland. They romped in fresh green, smelled the heady scent of bluebells, watched eggs hatch and baby birds emerge into the daylight. She even managed to produce a small deer, which let the children tiptoe towards it, before taking flight.

Numbers took on a life of their own and whizzed about playing the most extraordinary games. She discovered that fours could be very naughty but zeros were perfect for playing hoop-la. Shapes and colours were all great fun too. They built towers of bright cylinders and cubes, then bowled them over with fuzzy spheres that exploded, when they struck their targets, into showers of sparkling stars. The stars drifted up to become constellations in a dark blue sky. They floated up to join them, landing on the moon and bouncing, almost weightless, on its dusty surface. There they played races that had no beginning, no end, no winners. The children ran and hopped and chased until they were tired and ready for bed.

When they learned about the sea they went under the ocean in a see-through submarine and watched all the fish swimming in bright shoals. Until one little boy just stepped out of the submarine – through the wall – and swam with them. Once the children (and Sylvia) realised there was no need for a submarine it disappeared and they all swam, laughing and playing.

And, oh, how they loved the stories she shared with them. Stories about two little girls who were always getting into mischief, but ended each day tucked into bed by a smiling mother who kissed them both and wished them happy dreams. Somehow her mother's bedtime tales were in her head, word for word, and she enjoyed remembering them as much as the children enjoyed hearing them.

And so Sylvia taught them many facts about the world they had come from but slowly she began to see that it was the other things they were learning that really mattered. How to play with one another. How to treat each other gently and kindly. How to trust. Oh, that was a hard one. Gaining the trust of the shyer children, or those who had been traumatised, was especially rewarding. When a child like that finally climbed into her lap and hugged her, she knew what happiness was. And just as the Presence had said, children moved on. One day they would be there, the next ... gone. Slowly the numbers dwindled until there was only the little girl with the dark brown curls. Her solemn blue eyes would fix on her teacher from time to time as if she was waiting for something, expecting something from Sylvia. But she would never speak or say what she wanted. Then came a day when the Presence appeared. Holding out her hands to them she took them walking along a path that formed under their feet and faded away as they passed. They wandered around its curves and twists until they reached a deep pool. The surface was so still it was like a mirror. The Presence stopped there and let go of them.

'Well, Sylvia, you have been a good teacher to all those children. But I'm not sure if you've understood all *your* lessons yet.'

The Presence smiled and gestured toward the pool. The reflections of Sylvia and the little girl looked back, unwavering on the calm surface. The little girl seemed a bit older today. Taller. And Sylvia – well, she did a bit of a double-take. She looked so much younger.

Glancing back she exclaimed to the Presence,

'We're both changing. I was expecting my little pupil to grow up but I wasn't expecting to change myself too!'

'But that's exactly what Laura has been waiting for. For you to grow down.'

'Laura...?'

The not-so-little girl gripped Sylvia's hand and turned her back around to face the pool. Her reflection smiled as she spoke.

'Yes. Laura. Your sister. I've waited such a long time for you and now we can grow up together.'

As one reflection grew older and one raced back towards childhood the similarity was unmistakeable. Two young girls, identical in every respect, stood at the edge of the pool holding hands and smiling at each other. Somewhere, unseen, the Shining Presence watched as they ran off, laughing, to have the adventures they both deserved.

Seeing is believing

"Sight is a faculty; seeing is an art" George Perkins Marsh

There was no warning when Dan lost his sight. Well, okay, his eyes had been feeling a bit odd, hurting even, but he'd put that down to eyestrain. And there'd been a persistent headache aggravating him all week. He hadn't wanted to make a fuss about it because he'd already been off work for a few days with some kind of 'flu, so he'd swallowed headache tablets and waited for it to go away. All normal stuff really. But that night he'd gone to bed able to see and then he woke up blind. It was the biggest shock of his life. At first when he opened his eyes he assumed it was still the middle of the night. The room was in complete darkness. There wasn't even a glow from the light on the phone. Deciding he needed the bathroom, he reached for the pull-cord on the lamp, gave it a tug, heard it click, but….nothing. Damn. The bulb must have gone. He fumbled his way out of bed and felt for the door, and the light switch he knew was to the side of it. He stumbled over one of his slippers and scraped his hip against the corner of the chest of drawers but found his way finally to the wall. He slid his hands along till he got to the switch and turned it on. Again, nothing. Now he realised there must have been a power cut. That would explain the phone light being out too. And the fact that there was complete darkness with no orange-tinted glow from the streetlights to take the edge off things. Just then he heard his wife's voice.

'Dan? Are you all right?' She sounded puzzled.

'Fine, don't worry. It's probably a power cut. I'll have to find my way to the bathroom from memory. You go back to sleep. I expect the power will be back on by morning.'

'Dan?' Now she sounded.... well, scared....

'Dan, love, it *is* morning. I was just coming up to tell you to get a move on or you'll be late for work. Why are you switching all the lights on?'

It was Dan's turn to be puzzled. And a bit scared. Something was definitely not right.

'I haven't switched them on. I tried but the power's out.'

He felt his wife's hand on his arm.

'Come back to the bed. Let's sit you down and we can sort this out.'

He could hear a kind of restrained panic in her voice as she began to tug him away from the door. He realised that she seemed very confident about where she was going and let her lead him to the bed.

'Okay, now I want you to try to stay calm,' she said, in a far from steady voice, as she sat him on the edge of the bed, 'but I've got to tell you that it's broad daylight, the curtains are open, and yet you've been switching on the lamp and the main lights. And you've been stumbling around as if you've got your eyes shut. What can you see, Dan?'

'Nothing,' he whispered, horrified. 'There's nothing!'

He held a hand in front of his face. Waved it about. He could feel a draught of air but couldn't see a thing. He forced his eyes as wide open as he could. Still nothing. Karen got him to lie down again while she went to phone the doctor for advice. After being put through to the emergency number, she was told to call an ambulance. And so they had ended up at the hospital. On the way he kept straining to make out something, anything, screwing up his eyes and concentrating so hard he could feel the veins on his temples throb.

'Whoa, steady mate,' someone had said. 'Just try to stay calm till we can get you to a doctor. I know this must be a bit scary but just keep breathing slow and deep.'

His sleeve was rolled up and his blood pressure checked.

'It's a bit on the high side,' the voice informed him, 'but under the circumstances that's not surprising. Focus on your breathing and don't try to think about what's going on.'

Easier said than done. He had fought down the panic, wishing Karen had been able to come with him. She had stayed to drop the kids off at a friend's house but was going to follow on as quickly as she could. Not being able to see made him feel terrifyingly vulnerable. The world had become a very frightening place. He found himself listening to every sound he could hear over the engine noise, working out what it could be, where it was coming from. When they came to a stop and he was wheeled out on a trolley he could feel the transition from outdoors to indoors. There was a change in temperature, acoustics, the sound the trolley wheels made. He was being handed over to someone else and he could hear snatches of conversation. Voices were being kept low. Now why was that? This was happening to him, so surely he had a right to know. Anger and fear fought to come out on top. He heard something about 'bp'. He heard a mention of 'visual responses'. But that was it. He felt his eyelids being lifted, one at a time, and imagined a doctor shining a torch into them like they do on tv programmes. He wondered what response his eyes were giving the doctor because they were giving him nothing.

They carried out a number of tests before being certain of their diagnosis. He had been admitted and was propped in a hospital bed, Karen clutching hold of one hand, a drip inserted in the back of the other. A doctor was explaining what had happened. Dan concentrated on the voice, trying to label it in his mind to be sure he would recognise the doctor again. So much harder cataloguing and remembering a sound than a picture. It was a light voice, educated but not over-refined, and Dan felt the guy knew what he was talking about.

'There are a number of reasons why a person might suddenly lose his sight. There are some we could rule out immediately, such as trauma to the head caused by a heavy blow. Others are much more likely to affect one side of the head, and therefore one eye, or to have been preceded by a deterioration in sight. In your case we are certain it's been caused by an inflammation of your optic nerve – optic neuritis.'

He went on to explain the implications.

'First, the good news. It's treatable. We already have you on corticosteroids, which is an effective way to reduce the inflammation. When that happens you will almost certainly regain your sight.'

Dan felt relief flood through him and Karen's hand tightened on his. He heard a slight sniff and knew she would be trying to hold back tears. He squeezed back, then listened to the rest of the message. Apparently they couldn't tell when his sight would be back, two to three weeks was given as a guide. And there may well be long-term implications for his health, which they would monitor from now on, including the possibility of further occurrences and that his sight might not be quite as good as it had been. But he would see again! He clung to that thought, putting the rest to one side as a less-immediate concern.

After three days of intravenous drug treatment he was sent home with tablets to take for another week or so. It was a strange time for him and for everyone around him. Karen had warned him that Ben and Sam were more than a little upset by their father's sudden change. He tried to be sensitive to their feelings and to appear as confident as he could that his sight would return soon and everything would be normal. They'd been told they absolutely must not leave any toys out on the floor, or move any items of furniture around, otherwise dad might fall over it and hurt himself. But on his second day back Dan crashed to the floor when he tried to find his way from his armchair to the kitchen - only to walk straight into Ben who had stood, resolutely but silently, in front of him. The poor child was devastated at causing an accident.

'I'm sorry!' he'd wailed, tears spilling down his face, 'I thought if Dad had to get round me, he would see me. I thought it would make his eyes work again.'

It had taken a lot of reassurance to explain that no harm had been done and that, while they appreciated his efforts, it would be better to let the pills work instead. Eventually, after a couple of days, the boys got used to the situation. Now and then Dan would hear whispers and slight scuffling sounds around him. It was only when Karen caught them and told the boys off, that he found out they had been dancing around him pulling all sorts of faces then tiptoeing silently away to collapse in fits of giggles in the garden. Now he was aware of their game he became much more focused on what they were doing. He would pretend not to know they were there but would try to use any little noise or movement of air to fix their position in his mind. Then he would suddenly pounce with unerring accuracy, snatching up one of them, growling ferociously, while both boys shrieked and the one who hadn't been caught begged,

'Do me next, Dad!'

It was amazing how much he could pick up just by listening and sensing what was going on around him. He was much more tuned in to Karen's thoughts and moods than he would normally be. The slightest nuance in her voice would give him so much information. Suddenly he was earning all kinds of brownie points for being more considerate and sensitive, and realised that normally he didn't listen to half of what was said to him. Without visual distraction it was easier to concentrate.

Within a few days he was moving around the house more confidently and was even able to carry out tasks like making a cup of tea or a sandwich. He wasn't so good at clearing up after himself although, as Karen said, that was normal. But pretty quickly he started to feel cooped up. He couldn't watch tv or read the paper; he couldn't amble down to the pub for a swift half; he couldn't take himself off for a game of squash. And of course he couldn't drive. For someone who'd always lived life at 90 miles an hour, it was very confining. So his wife suggested they try walking to the park. It was only a couple of streets away and the roads were fairly free of traffic. They could link arms and walk along with the boys, looking like any other family out for a stroll.

Dan insisted on wearing his sunglasses as he didn't like the idea of other people being able to see him while he couldn't see them.

'It makes me feel exposed. Besides, if my gaze wanders in the direction of some gorgeous woman I don't want her to think I'm trying it on.'

Karen thought he'd attract more attention wandering about on a cloudy day wearing dark glasses but she dug out the pair he'd used on their last trip to France and, after dire warnings to the boys to stay very close and walk sensibly until they reached the park, they set off. It was slow and hesitant progress at first. Dan was shocked at how hard it was to put his trust in someone else until an exasperated Karen demanded to know if he really thought she was planning to walk him under a car or down a kerb without warning him. He took a deep breath, tried to release the tension he was feeling, and started to use a more normal stride and pace. Once he'd relaxed he was able to enjoy the sense of moving without being hemmed in by the dimensions of a room. The air was fresh and he could smell newly-mown grass, flowering shrubs, a faint whiff of cooking as they passed one particular house. He could hear the differences in their footsteps as they moved on different surfaces and past open areas or built-up parts. In his mind he was creating a map. It was not made up of lines and colours but of sound and smell.

The park was another fascinating experience. He sat on a bench while Karen took the boys to the play area. They were close enough that he could make out their voices but he was also able to listen to so many other sounds. There were many mysterious rustlings and snapping of twigs, he assumed from birds or small animals, and every so often footsteps would come along the path in front of him. To a casual observer he appeared to be sitting sleeping or deep in thought but actually he was intensely focused on his surroundings.

When they got back home he felt so much better for having escaped the house that he made up his mind to try to get out as often as possible. He knew Karen would take him when she could but it also gave a chance for the friends and neighbours to do something. They had all insisted that if there was anything they could do to help, 'just let me know'. Karen phoned a few and established a rota entitled Getting Dan Out From Under My Feet which she stuck to the fridge door. And so once, twice. or even more times a day someone would turn up to walk him to the park, the pub, a coffee shop. Even the library, after he was told about the talking book section. By the end of the second week he was feeling pretty good –

apart from the fact that he still couldn't see. Every day he was noticing more and more about the people and the world around him.

And then he started to feel the vibrations.

He called it that, 'the vibrations', because he didn't have any way to describe it to himself. He would suddenly become aware of something he couldn't possibly know about because he couldn't see it, and it wasn't something he could explain in terms of other senses. He knew, when he was standing near a grassy area, whether the grass was well-maintained or full of weeds; whether there was litter strewn around it; whether anyone was sitting there. He knew if Karen turned to look at him and what expression she had on her face. He knew when a bird hopped silently along the path in front of his favourite park bench. He knew that the car passing along the road was a particular colour. At first he thought he was imagining these things – after all, there was no way he *could* know, but he took to checking his impressions by asking innocent-seeming questions of whoever was with him.

Sitting on the park bench with Paul from two doors down he asked whether there were any squirrels around that day because 'Ben said there's always a squirrel in the tree opposite.'

He asked because he could feel very strongly the presence of a little grey squirrel. He had 'seen' it run up the trunk and now it was halfway along a branch, its paws to its mouth, nibbling on some small treat it had found. When Paul described the squirrel exactly as it appeared in his mind's eye Dan felt a shivery feeling move up his spine. It was so bizarre that for a moment he wondered if his sight was returning. He shut his eyes behind the dark glasses but he could still 'see' the squirrel as it suddenly raised its head, twitched its tail and dashed higher in the branches.

'What's it doing now?' he asked.

'It just ran up into the high branches,' Paul told him. 'It's out of sight now.'

Except that it wasn't. Dan knew exactly where it was. Even hidden among the leaves it couldn't escape from this special kind of sight.

It was difficult to figure out exactly what the difference was between this and 'real' sight. The nearest he got was by thinking about the difference between watching something on a tv or film screen, and seeing it live, but he also felt a strong connection to all the living things he saw in this way. From trees and plants, to small animals, and then his friends, neighbours, family. The sense of being connected to them was awe-inspiring. And, at times, so beautiful that he had tears in his eyes. He was grateful for his extra-dark lenses on more than one occasion.

For the next few days his family and friends were amazed at how well Dan was managing.

'Are you sure your sight hasn't come back?' Karen joked,' I'm beginning to think you're just hanging on for some extra time off work.'

He excused his new-found abilities by saying he'd heard something or felt a movement, and no-one caught on. He was glad about that. He didn't want anyone thinking he was delusional. And then, like a miracle, he began to get some normal vision. Quite blurry at first but then better and better. When he went for his check-up the doctor was pleased by the level of vision that had returned. Not quite 20:20 and his colour vision was a bit off, but a pretty good result.

And life got back to its usual routines. Dan was working again and had resumed his previous hectic lifestyle – with one exception. He found time to walk round to the park at least once or twice a week either with his family or on his own. He liked to spend a while sitting on 'his' bench. Just sitting quietly. Trying to recapture that special vision he'd known during his blindness. But the vibrations were gone. Now if he shut his eyes he had no sense of what was around him unless he could hear or touch it. He really missed that sense of connection with the world. Just knowing something was there by its vibrations, its energy. He wondered if he could bring it back by practising and started meditating while sitting there. He felt a bit daft at first so carried on wearing his dark glasses. Then, eyes closed, he'd try to find a peaceful place inside himself, clearing away any obtrusive thoughts. After trying for some weeks it was noticeable that he had become a much calmer person and his ability to concentrate had improved. Chatting privately to friends Karen would say how much easier he was to get on with since his illness. Meanwhile colleagues at work found him more approachable, much less aggressively competitive.

One Sunday morning, having walked to the newsagents to buy the papers, he returned home through the park and sat for a while in meditation. Time passed. Then he drew in a few deep breaths, ready to end the session and go home. That was when he saw the squirrel. He wondered if it might be the same one he'd 'seen' all those months ago and continued to sit as still as possible watching its antics. He heard footsteps approaching and recognised Paul coming along the path. With a bundle of newspapers under his arm he had obviously been on the same mission as Dan, who raised a hand in greeting. Paul joined him on the bench and they sat together enjoying the peace and quiet. After chatting for a while about the football, the weather, the football again, they made arrangements to join in the upcoming darts competition at The Crown. When he got to his feet, Paul leaned down to slap his neighbour lightly on the shoulder.

'Glad it's working out, mate,' he said, 'see you soon.'

'Thanks,' Dan called after him.

He swivelled back round to try to spot his favourite squirrel again but it had gone.

He sighed. Then, behind the dark lenses, he opened his eyes.

Shopping List

Matt decided his life had reached as low a point as any life could. There he was, a grown man, a man with a degree, a job, a flat... sitting in the doctor's waiting room and actually filling in one of those magazine quizzes. You know the kind. 'Are You A Seductive Temptress?' 'Are You Way Too Good For Him?' 'How Do You Know If He *Really* Likes You?'

The one that had somehow drawn him in was entitled 'Why Did He Leave You?' And it elaborated further, 'Are You Too Demanding or Not Demanding Enough? Take Our Fun Quiz and Find Out How To Hang On To Your Man'.

Okay, so he was straight, and more interested in hanging onto his woman, but even if Amanda's looks didn't exactly fulfil the criterion of 'he', Matt assumed the questions could be turned around to cover his situation. He couldn't just substitute 'she' for 'he' though. It took a bit of thought.

He had already decided that if his girl upset him he would prefer her to make up by sitting and talking it through, rather than pretending it hadn't happened, sulking and slamming doors, or turning up with a bouquet of roses. He had also come to the conclusion that a healthy relationship should rely on mutual honesty, not 'tact' or 'dressing up the truth'. But question 3 was proving tricky.

' Your guy comes in from work 2 hours late with a smug look on his face. Do you

(a) assume he's been to the pub with colleagues and beaten them at darts
(b) ask coyly if he's brought you a pressie
(c) demand to know if he's been with that bitch from Reception?'

Mentally he substituted shopping for the pub, and added 'got a bargain' instead of 'beaten them at darts'. He was completely stumped for an alternative for 'b'. And as for 'c' .... No he wouldn't have accused Amanda. He had known only too well that she was carrying on with his so-called friend Jamie. She wasn't exactly the most discreet cheater. After weeks of agonising over whether or not to confront her, of thinking that if he just stuck it out she'd tire of Jamie, the rug had been well and truly pulled from under him. She'd texted him. *Texted* for heaven's sake. While he was stuck at work. The message had been confusing. Probably, he'd concluded, the result of the use of abbreviations and predictive text.

> IM SOFT BT IM LEAKING U 2DAY PDBX IM LIKE TOTALLY GUSHING ILUVU BT ILUVJ MOR
>
> LJBF

It was quite a long text for Amanda and he didn't know if the confusions were solely due to predictive errors or her own lack of typing skills. Nor was he sure what the message was meant to say.

He got the office gofer to explain part of it, which meant that everyone knew within the hour that he'd been dumped. By text. What a loser!

Eventually he'd translated it as,

> *I'm sorry but I'm leaving you today. Please don't be cross.*
>
> *I'm like totally gutted. I love you but I love J more.*
>
> *Let's just be friends.'*

And when he got back to the flat that evening he discovered that Amanda had indeed left, having first done a more thorough job than your average break-in expert. Doors were flung wide open, drawers too; items she did not consider vital (his clothes, for instance) were strewn about; items of value were gone, regardless of who had bought them (mostly him), although the few gifts she'd bought for him had also gone. She'd even emptied the kitchen cupboards and the fridge of food and bottles of beer and wine. Perhaps, he thought glumly, she was planning to have a party when she got to Jamie's. The bathroom was a wreck. Obviously she had treated herself to some kind of spa day in there. It stank of things floral and it seemed every towel he owned was in the damp pile on the floor. The basin was stained with what he hoped was some sort of colour-your-hair-potion and his razor – oh, how he wished he'd gone electric – was in no fit state to return to his face. Right now Jamie was probably appreciating the smooth silkiness of Amanda's legs.

As he sorted out the chaos he tortured himself with thoughts of the two of them. Snuggling up, listening to *his* MP3, drinking *his* wine. Making a toast to their new life together. Amanda wearing that sexy underwear she'd made him buy even though he'd told her he couldn't really afford it. Arrrgh! So, giving up on the cleaning and tidying, he went down the road to the corner store, bought a six-pack and a bottle of wine and returned to the flat to drink himself into a stupor. Which he did so successfully that, when he eventually roused himself the next day, he didn't remember straight away that he was now a single man once again. He stumbled about the flat for a minute or two, looking for Amanda, till it all rushed back to his memory. At about the same time as the contents of his sorely-abused stomach rushed to their nearest exit.

When he phoned the office some time later to apologise for his non-appearance, common knowledge of his status as newly-dumped, together with the fact that he did sound truly terrible, got him a reprieve. And the suggestion that perhaps he should go to the doctor's as he didn't sound too good. He didn't of course. Just took headache tablets and slept off the hangover. But here he was, a couple of weeks later, waiting to see the doctor and hoping there was something available on prescription that could stop him lying awake night after night, tossing and turning, desperate to sleep. The face that had stared back from the bathroom mirror that morning had looked haggard and ten years older than it should. His eyes were bloodshot. His head felt dull and heavy. He was falling apart.

Frustrated by the quiz he sighed and tossed it back onto the centre table. It landed open, his scribbles clearly marking him as an 'A' personality. And the analysis of his shortcomings?

Are you a doormat? Have you forgotten the strength of your inner woman? Learn to appreciate her. Stand your ground. Expect greater things of your man and, if he can't deliver, find yourself a real man who can appreciate a real woman. Until you develop your self-esteem, you are asking to be dumped!

He lifted his gaze, lost in thought, and then his eyes met those of the woman who was also waiting her turn for an appointment. Startled, he looked away feeling hot colour creeping up his neck and then his face. It was bad enough he'd been caught reading a woman's magazine. Even worse to have filled in a quiz about hanging on to his man. Hastily he grabbed a copy of a car magazine and pretended to be absorbed in that. It was a relief when he eventually heard his name being called and was able to scuttle into the doctor's office.

Dr Talbot was sympathetic. But absolutely straight with him too.

'It's no good covering up whatever is eating away at you with pills,' he told Matt. 'If you need me to recommend you for counselling or advice, I'm happy to do that. Or you can just give the situation time. I'll let you have a two week supply of something that will relax you a little but I'm reluctant to prescribe anything stronger. See how you get on, but come back when you've finished these if there's still a problem.'

He had to accept, albeit grudgingly, that the doctor had probably been right. With the pills he was relaxed enough to get off to sleep each night though once he woke up he'd had it as far as any more rest was concerned. He took to getting up early and going for a run. He hadn't done that for years and was good to get moving. At 5 or 6 in the morning it felt as though the world was his private place. He nodded hello to a few of the now-familiar faces as he passed: the man at the corner shop just opening up, one or two regular dog-walkers, an occasional other runner. Spring was just arriving and he relished the freshness of the morning air and the simple pleasure of noticing trees beginning to build up blossom, or the bulbs that were opening all around the park and in people's gardens. He found himself looking forward to his runs and the way they made him feel afterwards. It was good to be getting back to peak fitness again. All those nights out with Amanda had taken their toll. He'd often yawned his way through each morning at work, fuelling on cups of strong coffee. She had never considered late nights to be a problem and could be out clubbing and pubbing till dawn, given the chance. And since he had always known that she would just go without him there had been a pressure to keep up with her. Letting her out of his sight for too long wasn't an option. The Amandas of this world wait for no man. Actually, he realised as he pounded along the path by the lake, it was a bit of a relief to admit that kind of lifestyle wasn't really his thing. All the noise, the booze, having to watch out for Amanda all the time. He could never relax and just enjoy himself.

At work he was much more attentive to what he was doing. More efficient too. And it didn't go unnoticed. His annual development meeting with his immediate boss went very well and he was given a small pay increase. His heart had taken a battering but suddenly everything else in his life was going smoothly. Maybe, he thought, he just wasn't cut out for a serious relationship.

That attitude lasted for all of a week before he finally admitted to himself that he did want another relationship. Not just short-term either. He was ready for the full monty – marriage, a home, a family. Everything that was the antithesis of his time with Amanda. So he started trawling through internet sites with the idea of trying some on-line dating. Maybe it would be the equivalent of dipping his toe in the water. Get to know someone digitally then go for a face to face meeting. He could weed out any high-maintenance types like Amanda and find someone who really wanted to commit to a future with him. He chose a dating site that didn't look too scary and filled in his on-line questionnaire. He was as honest as he could be about himself and was more than happy to submit an up-to-date photo now he was looking fitter. The stumbling block was in trying to describe the woman he would like to be with. He screwed his eyes tight shut and tried to visualise his ideal woman. Tall? Short? Skinny? A bit plumper? Blonde? Brunette? His age? Younger? Maybe he should be looking for an older woman? Should she have a high-powered career or something a bit less pressured? What about her politics or religion or hobbies? Good sense of humour? Damn, why would anyone write that? Were there people going around saying 'I have no sense of humour whatsoever. I never laugh or smile unless it's at something totally inappropriate that no-one else finds amusing'? He didn't think so. Everyone thinks they have a great sense of humour. Scrub that thought. How about describing the kind of interests he'd like her to have?

It was hopeless. Nothing came to him. Sighing, he hit the delete button without submitting his application. It wasn't worth continuing until he had a clearer idea of what he was looking for.

Later that week he was in a meeting at work. He was listening with one ear, because he didn't think it wasn't anything complicated or interesting, and doodling on a notepad. He held the pad at an angle to make it seem as if he could be taking notes although he knew everyone else would be doodling. Or writing their shopping lists. Then a thought struck him. He should make a shopping list for the perfect woman. And never mind about the stuff people usually write about looks or hobbies. How would his ideal partner deal with something boring, like this meeting? He turned over the page of the pad as quietly as he could and wrote:

1 My ideal woman would deal with a boring situation honestly and bluntly. She would just say 'This is boring. Can we do something else?' But if I'm the one being boring she'll tactfully turn me aside from it, distract me, or make me smile. And I will know she's being kind and feel a warm glow about it, appreciating her tact. But I'll also stop doing the boring thing. Whatever it is. That's how two people learn to modify their behaviour so they become a couple not just two people sharing a home.

He read it through silently and nodded to himself. Then at the top of the page he wrote: 'Shopping List for my Ideal Woman'.

Martin who was leading the meeting had seen the nod and paused in his delivery.

'Is there a thought you need to add there, Matt?'

Matt raised his head and said with sincerity,

'I think I've really learnt something here, Martin. Thank you.'

One or two others sniggered to themselves, assuming he was being sarcastic, and Martin flushed with embarrassment, unsure whether he was being complimented or made fun of.

'Could you clarify that?' he asked.

Matt though for a second or to then said,

'Really it's all about working together, looking out for each other, seeing the best in what the other person does and encouraging them to be even better. That way we can build something worthwhile.'

With that input Martin felt his talk about 'Leadership Teams in the Business Context' had really got through. Not only did it give him a boost of confidence, which galvanised the rest of his talk quite noticeably, but later that day he also put in a good word about Matt with their boss.

'He really got it,' he enthused, 'and I think it spurred the others on to hear how he supported it.'

Oblivious to the impact his remarks had caused, Matt was back at his desk and adding to his list whenever an idea came to him.

2 My ideal woman would be a good negotiator. She would understand the importance of compromise. She would realise that neither of us should get our own way all the time but that both of us should be prepared to gain some of what we want but also give up some of it. For instance, if I decided I wanted to take up golf she might decide to do it too so that we spend time together, or she might get me to agree limits on when I play and arrange to go to zumba classes at that time, so we're both doing things we want but not all the time. Time apart is good but not too much otherwise we lose what matters about our partnership.

3 We would discuss the important things we want from our relationship and work together to achieve them. Whether it's a decision about a home, a family, travel abroad, our ambitions. You can't be one-sided about the big stuff in life or it doesn't work. Like with Amanda, when I wanted a home and marriage and children but she wanted to go out clubbing every night and sleep with Jamie. We have to communicate.

He paused at that one, realising with some surprise that it didn't hurt him to think about Amanda. He could see now that they'd never had the important talks. He'd just assumed she'd come round to his way of thinking eventually if he could hang on long enough. And she'd just gone on doing what she wanted, assuming *he* would realise she was a free spirit and that she was only there till something better came along. Even Jamie wouldn't last, he thought. Sooner or later a better prospect would appear and Jamie would go the way of all Amanda's men.

Shortly after he wrote:

4 My ideal woman would be a sticker, like me. Not giving up when things get difficult but trying again and again. If we both have that attitude then if one of us gets to a dark place the other one will still be fighting to keep our partnership alive.

He turned back to his work, deciding to put in a bit of extra time that evening. He was conscious of the fact that he'd spent much of the afternoon thinking about his life and not the job in hand, and he honestly liked his work He was putting more into it but seemed to be getting more back. So, he thought, an hour or two on this project should sort out the main snags and he could leave it on Mr Richardson's desk ready for the morning. It was nearer three hours before he was satisfied and most of his colleagues had long since left. He stretched and yawned, then gathered up his belongings. Heading for the boss's office, he almost bumped into him rounding the corner. Dennis Richardson had just fetched a coffee and was planning to work on. They chatted briefly as Matt handed over the report he'd been working on.

'Thank you for this,' said Dennis, looking impressed, 'I'll give it a look over this evening. I hope you're not turning into a workaholic like me? Ulcers aren't a good option.'

Matt grinned.

'No sir, it's just that I wanted to finish this. I got stuck into it and it would have been more work to stop and then pick up the threads again tomorrow than just plough on. Besides I'm between relationships at the moment...'

'Ah, no pretty girl at home waiting for you?'

'No sir,' said Matt turning to go, 'but I'm working on it!'

As he got into his car he paused before starting the engine. Then he fished out the notepad and wrote:

5 We need to work at our relationship but there has to be fun too. Otherwise what's the point? I'd like it if we made each other laugh, and feel safe, and loved. I'd like it if we could be proud of each other. I'd like...

He paused and thought, then wrote

I'd like to be happy to come home and looking forward to sharing each other's day.

'That's it,' he said out loud, 'that list says it all!'

He tore the sheet out of the pad, folded it and tucked it into his pocket. Next time he thought that he'd met the right woman that list would come out and he would check her against it, point by point.

Heading home he decided to stop and get a few bits and pieces at the supermarket on the main road. It was open till eleven but tended to be very quiet after about eight. He preferred to shop then, wandering up and down the aisles in peace. No screaming kids. No people pushing and shoving. No queues at the checkouts. You just had to be prepared to work your way around the shelf-stackers who tended to block most of each aisle with huge trolleys of goods to set out.

He drifted along, humming under his breath, dropping items into his basket. He felt very satisfied with himself. He'd put in a good day at work, and he'd sorted out what he wanted next in life. The perfect woman to settle down with. Smiling happily he headed off to the checkout. He chatted briefly to the woman on the till as she checked his shopping through and packed it in a plastic bag for him. He thanked her and wished her a good evening, then headed home.

It was a week later that he popped into his local supermarket again for his usual Friday evening shop. Dennis Richardson had called him into the office for 'a little chat about his future with the company'. He said that Matt had come to his attention as good management material. The company wanted to put him on track for a senior position and there were going to be extra training opportunities in the next six months, followed by a promotion. Matt was grinning from ear to ear as he left and he decided to call in and buy a steak and a very special bottle of wine to celebrate. Unfortunately it would be a solitary celebration. In spite of the fact that his work life was going so well, his social life was still non-existent. He'd phoned his parents to tell them the news and they were at least as thrilled as Matt, if not more so. He was going back for a visit at the weekend, having been promised a big roast dinner – his parents' version of the fatted calf. But for tonight he'd celebrate alone. He paid and picked up his bag then carried on to his flat. As he unpacked a piece of paper dropped out. He picked it up, expecting to find a promotional leaflet. Instead it was a plain sheet of paper with some typed words:

Looking for the ideal woman? Well, maybe she's here.

My ideal man would be someone who saw marriage as a challenge. Someone who accepts that both parties have to change their behaviour. So many men think they can carry on just as they did before they married whilst so many women seem to accept that they have to give ground on everything, losing the identity that attracted the man in the first place. But I think you and I have really got to grips with no. 1. Don't you? I'm giving you a big tick for this one. Score one.

Matt stood, shocked and bemused. It was as though someone had read his mind. Someone knew his list! Then he grabbed his jacket from the back of the chair and began frantically rifling through the pockets. The list wasn't there. He knew he'd put it in the inside pocket, next to his wallet. His wallet…. maybe when he'd pulled out his wallet somewhere he'd dropped the list. But who had picked it up? And, more importantly, who had replied? He racked his brain to think how the message could have got there. The woman at the till hadn't packed his bag for him today. He'd taken the bag from the pile and put his shopping in himself. However, there had been someone near the door who had collided with him briefly. They had both said a quick 'sorry' and he'd stepped back to let her through the door, but all he had now was an impression of dark hair, a beige mac. Maybe heels? Or boots? It was like having a stalker – someone who was watching him, who knew what he'd been thinking about. But whoever she was remained a mystery to him. He wasn't sure how he felt about it.

It was just a couple of days before he ventured back to the supermarket – he wasn't leaving it till Friday - and it was a very different Matt who went around putting things in his basket this time. He was hyper-vigilant, holding tightly to the handle, eyes swivelling in every direction. Every time he caught a glimpse of someone with dark hair, he did a quick check. Was it the woman who had bumped into him? He couldn't be sure, but there were a couple of possible candidates in the store that evening. He tried making eye contact with each of them but they looked through him. And the second one, he noticed, was wearing a wedding ring. He headed for the checkout, dispirited and a bit lost as to what to do next. The usual woman was on the till so he mustered a smile and said hello. She asked him if he'd found everything he wanted, and he laughed ruefully.

'Not quite,' he told her, 'I was on the look-out for something a bit special tonight.'

'Anything I can help with?' she asked brightly.

He shook his head.

'No, sorry, I don't think the store stocks what I was after.'

'Never mind,' she consoled him, 'at least you've got one of these.'

She handed him a money-off coupon along with his receipt. He glanced at it before tucking it into the bag with his shopping.

As he unpacked the makings for a spag bol supper a note fluttered to the floor. He picked it up with a mixture of trepidation and excitement.

Hey! Negotiation? I'm with you there. When two people are trying to build a life together they carry with them all their previous experiences, both good and bad. That will guide all their future decisions. But of course that will point them in different directions. How can they resolve their different viewpoints? And head off into the same sunset? Of course they need to negotiate. I'm giving you a second tick because that works for me.

Dammit! How had she done it? He was torn between feeling frustrated and having a sense of admiration for this mystery woman's ability to sneak messages to him. He decided to test her preparedness and headed back to shop again the next Friday. He'd worked late again, finishing up various jobs in preparation for a course he was going on the next week. He wanted to leave a clear desk and empty in-tray. So he wondered if she would still be there. Maybe she was another shopper, or maybe an employee. Perhaps tonight he'd suss her out. But nothing untoward happened at any point around the supermarket. There was a different woman on the till, not as friendly as the other one, and he arrived home feeling slightly let down. Maybe his mystery woman had tired of the game. Or maybe she didn't think he'd be back so soon. He started to unpack the bag, then stopped. On the back of the cereal packet was a piece of paper, held on by a couple of small strips of tape.

Okay, communication. Let's get straight to the point. I've wasted a large part of my twenties involved with men who are happy to settle for a girlfriend but really aren't looking for anything too permanent. I've waited around hoping the penny will drop and they'd realise all they wanted was to put a ring on my finger and live in connubial bliss. Eventually they've fallen out of love/lust/patience and decided to end things. Or I have. So now I've found someone who's open to honest communication I'm going to put my cards on the table. The actual marriage stuff isn't a deal-breaker. What I want is commitment, and children, if we're able to have them. Everything else is open for negotiation, (please refer to previous note). So it seems we're still on the same page. I'm giving you another tick.

How? How was she doing it? No-one came near him as he shopped. He'd been very careful to keep a constant watch. He'd passed a few people on shelf-stacking duty. There'd been a young boy on the checkout. No-one had bumped into him. It was driving him crazy. He thought back to his list. What had he put for number four? It was something to do with perseverance. Huh. She'd got that one in the bag already.

He froze, thinking it through. In the bag already. Maybe that was it? The message was in the bag before his purchases went in? He tried to remember. The first note... The woman on the till hadn't packed it for him. But maybe the note was already in the bag as she saw him approach the till. He'd taken a bag from the pile. Ah yes, she'd done that usual thing of opening bags and tossing them down the loading area. He had just picked up the top bag, the last one she opened. Could it have had a message in? A message he hadn't noticed as she chatted to him? What about the second note? He thought hard. She handed him a receipt and a flier, something about money off. He'd taken a quick look then stuffed it into the bag. Supposing the note was behind the flier? That could have worked. He started to feel excited. He was sure he'd got it right. Now, the third time... Hmmm....She hadn't been on the till. Hang on though, could she have been elsewhere in the store? Perhaps stocking shelves? He knew no-one had come near his basket but perhaps it was like the 'already in the bag' trick. Maybe the message was already on the cereal box. Though how could she have known he would pick up the box? Unless.. oh yes... he always bought a box of that brand. He was definitely a creature of habit when it came to the weekly shop. And he'd been heading towards that aisle. It would only have taken a second or two to pop the message on the box at the front of the pile. And if he hadn't picked it up, why, she could have slipped back and removed it, waiting for a better opportunity to pass it on.

He wondered what to do about his theory. Should he pretend he hadn't worked it out? Or should he confront her? Ah, but what if he'd got it wrong? He started to obsess about the situation. She had always seemed so pleasant and friendly. He really could see himself getting to know her better. But he didn't even know her name or anything about her background.

He stopped and reconsidered. Actually he knew a lot of very important things about her. He knew that she shared many of the same views as him and that she expressed her views in a clear and articulate way. She had a sense of humour, albeit slightly quirky! She was looking for a long-term relationship. She was resourceful. He decided to take a leap of faith and started working on his own cunning plan.

It wasn't till late on the following Friday evening that he ventured back. He didn't bother picking up a basket but headed straight for the only open till. She was there.

'Hi,' he said, glancing at her name badge. 'Hi, Marie, I wonder if you could help me?'

'What do you need?' she asked with a warm smile.

'I have an ad I'd like to put on the community board. Is there a charge?'

'Not for regular customers like you,' she replied, 'would you like me to put it up for you?'

'Thanks!'

Matt handed over his carefully-worded ad then turned and walked out of the store. As he left Marie looked down at the paper he'd given her.

WANTED

LOST SHOPPING LIST

REWARD FOR SAFE RETURN

(SUPPER AT CASA ROSSA)

PLEASE PHONE TO ARRANGE A TIME

His phone number followed. Marie grinned then fished out from under the counter the other two notes she'd prepared. She didn't think they'd be needed now.

Acting Out

I know murder is wrong. To take the life of another person just isn't acceptable even by today's lax standards. But what if that person has taken your life? Not literally, but in every other way. What if he (for I am, of course, meaning my darling husband of thirty something years), what if he has blighted your entire life? Depriving you (and by you I do, of course, mean me) and the world of a talent that should have been expressed? Denying me my rightful status and dragging me down to the depths of dreardom? Under such circumstances isn't murder more like ... justice?

My life should have been so different. I had a place at RADA you know, back in 1978. The same year as Kenneth Branagh and Paul McGann. And I was destined for the same route to stardom. I'd even changed my name from Geraldine Mitchell to Stella Mitchel in anticipation of my glittering future. Stella because it means 'star', as I'm sure you realise, and Mitchel with one 'l'. I think that makes it stand out more, don't you? It's a bit of a talking point for interviews with reporters from glossy magazines. 'That's Ms Mitchel with one 'l', dear. But do call me Stella!' Flash a bright smile. Watch them succumb to my star-like charm. So full of grace and sheer star quality that the image dazzles even me.

But I'm here. In the dark. Alone. There's no pain, for which I'm grateful. I do think pain causes dreadful wrinkles. And a very *pinched* look to the face. It's just not attractive, is it? Now, *playing the part* of someone suffering a tragic, incurable illness ... well, that gives such scope for making the audience cry as they fall in love with your sad, doomed character. And if you can do it whilst sitting in a wheelchair so you can allow your blanket to slip slightly to the side, revealing shapely but sadly lifeless legs, so much the better. There's usually a strong manly lead who has to lift you from the chair at some point, while you rest your beautiful head against his chest, your pale face showing such courage as you gently bite your bottom lip against the imaginary agony, and your artfully made-up eyes gazing gratefully up at his handsome profile. That's the sort of part I was born to play. There's nothing very uplifting about pain though. So all in all the fact that I'm feeling nothing means I'm putting that down as a bit of a plus. There's no heat or cold either. No sensation of lying on anything, touching anything. I can't see. I can't move. Believe me, I've tried, but there's nothing at all. Apart from my hearing. That's the only way I know where I am, and why. I can hear everything. Except for the times when I go somewhere else. Perhaps I sleep though I have no sensation of tiredness. After an interval back I am, in the dark, listening to all their comments and conversations. By which I know I've been away. Discussions have moved on. The people have changed. So many gaps – I wonder what I'm missing out on.

When I first became aware of being here I thought there was an elderly asthmatic nearby. Oh, it was *so* aggravating! I wanted to shout 'Be quiet! Have some consideration!' but I couldn't make a sound. Instead all I could hear was gurgle-suck-wheeze-gasp. Gurgle- suck-wheeze-gasp. Then, by listening to the chatter of people I assume to be nurses, I discovered it to be the sound of a ventilator. One that was keeping me alive. Breathing for me. Not that I can feel the rise and fall of my chest. Such a shame. I've always loved performances that allow me to heave my bosoms, preferably whilst wearing a tightly-fitting, low-cut dress. Oh, to be Lady Hamilton again, spilling over the top of my gown, straining toward Napoleon as he reaches for me lustfully. Or should that be Nelson? I'm never quite sure. Still, I looked so gorgeous in that gown I *insisted* we did a play about Nell Gwynn the next year. I think they were won over by my argument that it would save the cost of a new dress. I don't mind thrift when it involves vintage silk and lace. I think I ended up taking it home to clean after the last performance of 'Squeeze My Oranges', but I can't recall if it ever got back to the Easington Players. That's Easington in the Home Counties. I'm not sure they do Amateur Dramatics in the far north of England.

'Amateur' means lover of something. Did you know that? Amateur actor. Lover of the dramatic arts. That's what I am. I always had a flair for the stage, even as a child. Then by my teens it had become a passion. I tried twice to get into RADA but even with Daddy's friend pulling a few strings, it wasn't easy. It was so thrilling the first day I stepped through the door. First, there would be the excitement of learning my craft in such a prestigious setting. That would be followed by a few smaller parts - I expected the stage would be the perfect vehicle for me, though I wouldn't object to a little tv work – followed by stardom, once a discerning agent discovered me. Bliss. My whole life was mapped out beautifully. Then Douglas came along, folded up the map, along the wrong creases, and stuffed it into the glovebox of an ordinary life.

I'm quite pleased by that analogy. Or is it a metaphor? Anyway I'm impressed by the car reference – so appropriate since Dougie was, at the time, a garage mechanic. Not that I realised when I met him.

Some of the students used to frequent a dive of a pub just around the corner. We didn't have much money for drinking but you could make a half of shandy go quite a long way. He was there, in the corner, eying me up. I have to admit he was quite a looker back then, with his dark, brooding eyes and his black curls. Hair like David Essex, he had. And tall. Just imagine Heathcliff walking over to you and you'll know why I let him buy me a proper drink (I *insisted* on a gin and tonic even though I didn't like the taste – so much more sophisticated than shandy. And I think it sets the tone. Makes it clear that you're a lady and expect to be looked after properly). Well we chatted a bit and that's when he told me he was a mechanic. I assumed he meant he was doing one of the non-actor courses. Stagehand stuff. I don't know. I didn't have any interest unless it happened in front of the curtain and in the glare of the spotlights. He certainly had more money than most of the students who'd been after me. And he had a bedsit of his own. I was quite impressed at the time. Less so when I found out he worked at Jim's Cars and Repairs. Unfortunately, by that time, I'd got used to having a boyfriend who could take me out to proper dates at the cinema or local restaurants. He had a car too, and what with that and the bedsit there were plenty of opportunities for a young, sexy, actress-to-be to get into a spot of bother. The sex was good. Getting pregnant, not so good.

Daddy was furious and Mummy was *incandescent*. They made it quite clear I should get rid of the child and get back to my studies. After all the money I'd cost them for acting lessons and stage school. I had been so insistent that I wanted a career on the stage. But Dougie got down on one knee and proposed. We were in the middle of learning about Stanislavski's system at the time, 'Make it *live*, Stella. Make me *believe!*' And I was finding it all a bit tedious, so I thought, why not marry Dougie? Maybe I could get back to RADA after the birth and they'd be on to something more my style.

It never happened. The baby arrived – by Caesarean, you know my views on pain – a screwed-up bundle of wailing anger, leaking noxious matter from every orifice. I didn't really take to the whole motherhood thing but my parents had a sudden change of heart when they saw their grandson. Naming him Walter after Daddy helped a lot, though I don't think it helped *him* when he got to school with all the Waynes and Pauls and Aarons. Daddy supported us in getting a small flat and Mummy was there almost constantly, seeing to Baby Walter's more mundane needs. Meanwhile Dougie worked long hours at two jobs to keep me in an appropriate lifestyle. He soon learned how to treat a lady like me! He was keen to make our family bigger once we could afford it so as soon as I could, I scraped together money from various birthday and Christmas gifts (always ask for receipts then take them *straight* back and swap for cash, or sell them – I'm rather a fan of Ebay these days) then I took myself off to a small private clinic and had my tubes tied. I told Dougie I needed a small rest to recover from the birth and the subsequent stress of motherhood, and since I'd already been recovering for the best part of a year so far, he accepted my cover story of a quiet stay in a hotel. He paid for the 'hotel' bill and added extra money in case I wanted to treat myself. Sweet. When no more babies arrived he would mutter sometimes about getting ourselves checked out. I just encouraged him to 'give it a bit more time'. I think in the end he got resigned to having just the one.

I never did get back to RADA. With Daddy's backing Dougie had taken over a garage of his own and had built up a thriving business. By the time Walter was off to school he had two more and we had moved out of London to our beautiful house in Easington. I made it clear we would need an au pair to look after Walter so he wouldn't seem deprived to the other children at his private school. Marta dropped him off before school, picked him up after, took him to his football training and his piano lessons. She washed his clothes and packed his lunches and nursed him when he was ill. The rest of the time it was down to me. The house was too large for me to cope with that as well so we had a gardener and a cleaner. Managing the staff was pretty much a full-time job but you have to stay on top of them or they get lazy.

So no, I never got back to my studies, and being a full-time mother meant I couldn't break into acting any other way. I would look at Walter sometimes and think, was it worth it? Giving up on my talent to rear this child? And I would think, no. Definitely not. I just didn't take to him, you see. Particularly once he got to that awful spotty, slouchy, voice-dropping stage. Perhaps if he'd been a girl...we'd have gone shopping for clothes together when she was a teenager and people would mistake us for sisters. She would laughingly tell people I was her closest friend. I could picture it clearly. Oh, we'd look so good in photos. Yes, I honestly think a girl would have been all right. Not this graceless lump.

Dougie had aged rapidly by the time our son was in his teens. Who would have expected that attractive Heathcliff look-alike to turn into a balding tubby by his mid-thirties! I used to say to him, you have to make an effort and look after yourself. Do you think my looks just happen? No! It takes *hours* of attention to keep my skin, hair, nails looking this good. I *try*, Dougie, so why don't you? He took to spending longer at the office and I was glad for the extra peace and quiet. Mind you, the evenings could seem a bit lonely at times so when I heard somebody was setting up a local AmDram group I was *thrilled!* They were running auditions in the local church hall, but as I said when Dougie drove me there, I did a stint at RADA so I don't think you'll need to audition *me*. And they didn't. Especially when Dougie offered to sponsor their first production. That was how he got involved too. First of all with backing. Then he started to take over the group's books and made it profitable. After he'd had his heart attack and sold up the businesses, he had plenty of time on his hands to help with backstage work. Working with his hands again seemed to do him good and his paunch slowly disappeared. That was when I noticed him smiling and laughing a lot more. Once or twice I spotted him hanging around a lot with that dreadful Alice who sewed the costumes. We'd tried to get her to fill in for a small walk-on part once but it was hopeless. The girl just went bright red and stuttered. Said she was happier behind the scenes – idiot! Even Dougie managed more than that and had worked up to taking on small parts in our productions. Well, he could chat and flirt all he wanted, if it kept him out of my hair, but I could see I'd need to mark young Alice's card for her if things went too far. Admittedly, I'd had the odd fling but it's so hard for a woman of my sensuality and artistic temperament, living with a boor like Dougie. A boor, and a bore. I'd laugh at that if I could – such a clever play on words.

Meanwhile I continued to wow audiences with regular leading roles. As I'd edged up through my forties I had occasionally relinquished these to other actresses, favouring the sort of brief cameo appearance Dame Judy also does so well. Fewer lines to learn, but you can still steal the show and the hearts of the audience.

Can you hear those voices? That's my pathetic excuse of a husband. I think the other man is some sort of consultant. He's explaining that there's no sign of brain activity. Well, for heaven's sake, you can't get more active than this! I know my brain is *whirling* with activity but I can't move or speak or cry, so how do I let them know? It's a problem, isn't it? Imagine their expressions if I gently uncurled the fingers of one hand, right now, and made a sort of little breathy sigh, then opened my eyes. Perhaps a single tear could overflow the bottom lid and trickle slowly down my pale cheek. Dougie would reach out to wipe it away with his hairy paw but I think the consultant would get there first. I'm sure he has long, sensitive fingers, neatly manicured. 'Welcome back, Stella,' he says softly, 'we thought we'd lost you.' If Dougie weren't in the room he might even lean across and place a chaste kiss on my unlined brow. Oh, how easily I could play that part! It's so frustrating not to be able to do it just the way I can see it in my head.

But I was telling you about Dougie and the idiotic Alice. Oh, did I mention her stringy hair? SHE CUTS IT HERSELF!!! There, I knew you'd be horrified. What kind of woman DOES that. Really! I've never seen her with eyeliner or a smart outfit. And her chest is definitely not the heaving kind - I've got dimples that are bigger. But there she was, smiling up at my husband, letting him whisper in her ear when they thought no-one was looking. God knows, I can't stand the man any more but I am his wife and the mother of his son. I was in such a temper that night when we got home that I confronted him. And he didn't deny it. He had the gall to claim they were 'in love'. Oh, somebody pass the sick bag. Fifteen years younger than him! I shouted, 'You realise she's only after your money?' And, do you know what he said? He turned to leave the room and as he went I heard him mutter, 'No, that's you.'

Well, I screamed at him to get back but I heard him go upstairs and lock himself in his bedroom. We'd had separate ones for several years now. His footsteps moved overhead then I could hear the bath running. Stunned, I sat down to think. He hadn't mentioned divorce but that was one short step away. A thought struck me and I crept off to the study to go through his desk. The diary on top had appointments listed with Macready and Bagley, local solicitors but not our usual firm. I went cold. After all my years of sacrifice was he planning to discard me? And for a younger woman? Hell, she could probably still have children. They could start a family. And where would that leave me? I wanted to *kill* him! I wanted to stab him, drown him, push him off a cliff. I wanted to shoot him, just like in the play we'd been rehearsing…

Now there was an idea.

In the play he was a lover who betrayed me. (And they say theatre isn't like real life – hah!) In the final scene I raised a gun and fired a blank at him across the stage. He would slump to the floor bleeding. Then after a heart-rending speech about not being able to live with his betrayal but not being able to live without him, I would raise the gun, point it at my head and fire again. I do so love a death scene. At my peak I could 'die' for a full five minutes. Now I know what you're thinking – you fire even a blank that close and you could kill yourself. Stagecraft, my dear. Only one blank would be loaded in the gun, for 'shooting' Dougie. When I fired the second time I would use a little device to issue some realistic-looking smoke while someone off stage provided the 'bang'.

Supposing somebody swapped the blank in the gun for real ammunition? I'd seen those tv shows about fingerprints and suchlike. I knew you'd have to avoid getting fingerprints on the bullet. The gun wouldn't matter as people would expect it to have my prints. Now where could I get a bullet? That was actually quite easy and I was so pleased when I worked it out. Daddy used to belong to a gun club and, after he died, Mummy had kept all of his old things in the attic. I could have a look up there on the pretext of finding something of Daddy's that I wanted to give to Walter. And if I took a blank I could see if there was a similar size bullet. I assumed they would be like dress sizes, so If I matched them the real bullet ought to fit the stage gun. Mummy was so senile these days she probably wouldn't even remember I'd been there. So that's what I did. And for the special performance and Dougie's demise I chose the dress rehearsal, when the group's members invited a few friends and family to sit in the audience. Walter was there, with his latest girlfriend. I did wonder for a moment whether I should put it off till the full performance but a boy's got to lose his father sometime, hasn't he? Backstage the gun was in my dressing-room since it was a prop for me to carry on. I managed to open the gun, removed the blank, and put in a real bullet. I hid the blank behind some old books stacked in the corner. Then, leaving the door open, I left the room. No-one else had a private place to change so they were all milling about. I made my presence obvious by stopping to chat to various members of the cast, passing on titbits of acting advice. All this was my alibi you see. If the police could prove I was the only one with access to the gun, they'd know I'd done it. Now I was making it possible for anyone to slip in there and do the deed.

Most of the play was a blur. I was so focused on reaching the final scene that I perhaps didn't give my best performance. The moment came. Dougie the betrayer turned his back to leave me, and I raised the gun, screamed my line, and fired. Bang! Such a loud noise in a small theatre. As planned, Dougie slumped to the floor. The fake blood was spreading across his back. Only I knew that real blood was mingling with it. Even if the shot didn't kill him outright, by the time I'd finished dying, it would be too late for him. And if he made groaning noises people would just assume he was hamming it up, stealing my thunder. But he just lay there. As I launched into my last speech I had thoughts of selling up the house, cashing in our investments, and maybe buying a villa in Spain. Or Tuscany...

'...but I cannot live without you, even though you would have left me! Oh, Patrick, my darling... why? ...why?'

I pulled the trigger. Bang! The next conscious thought I had was here. And still I don't know 'why'.

There have been more voices in and out today. It's clear to me now that I have suffered a major head injury. Thank god the rest of me must be looking as good as usual. I'm picturing some bandaging, a few tendrils of hair creeping loose to lie across the pillow, my pale face dignified and composed. They still don't think I'm inside here though, and they have no idea I can hear them. The machines are keeping me breathing, keeping me fed. And over and over I think about the events of that evening, on stage, and wonder how this happened. I hear more voices coming near. I can pick out Dougie…Walter…and, is that Mummy? Oh good, I think my dishy consultant is here again. I do hope that when I'm back to normal he lives up to my imagination!

'I realise that it's been a hard decision but you must understand you are doing the right thing.'

Such an earnest voice. I'm sure he'd be a wonderful lover.

'Thank you for that. It's a comfort to know you're so sure. Perhaps we could say our goodbyes?'

'Yes of course, take as long as you need.'

I hear steps going away and the door closing with a gentle click. I'm confused. What decision? Are they moving me to a private clinic or something? Maybe they've given consent for an operation. Or a second opinion…

'Me first, Dad.'

A pause. I hear Walter clear his throat, then,

'You've never been a mother to me or a wife to dad so I guess we won't miss you. I'm not even sorry you got hurt and I'm not going to pretend I am. And I think that's all I want to say to you.'

'Oh Walter!'

Mummy's voice. She should be sounding angry with him. Not *sorrowful*. How dare he speak to me in this way, even if he doesn't know I can hear him.

'It's all right gran, I always had you and granddad, as well as dad. I've done all right.'

A sigh.

'She was a bright, lively child but she just grew into this self-absorbed monster. Maybe it was our fault. We always indulged her... Maybe...'

I could hear her come nearer to me. She was choking back sobs.

'I'm sorry if we failed you dear. We wanted so much for you but I think, now, that we got it all wrong...'

The sobs took over.

'Shhh... it's OK, gran. It wasn't your fault. She made her choices. Let's go out and leave dad in peace to say his goodbyes.'

I'm struggling to say something, tell them they've got it all wrong. I'm trying so hard to move, to do something, that my head feels like it could explode. Nothing happens. I'm held like a... like a fly in a web. And I am so frightened! Why are they saying these things? They're trying to tie me down with petty restrictions and expectations, but I'm *special*. I've always been special. And special people can't be expected to follow the same rules as the sheep around them.

They've had the privilege of living in my aura, of basking in my light. They *adore* me, I know they do.

That's the door closing. Footsteps coming towards me. I can hear breathing. He must be bending down to speak in my ear...

'You are a hateful, selfish bitch and any minute now we're going to pull the plug on you. I do hope you can hear this because it's not the way you planned, is it? You should be standing by my grave looking forlorn but dignified in a black designer suit, dabbing at fake tears with a lace-edged handkerchief. What could have gone wrong?'

Exactly. What the *hell* went wrong?

A laugh. It doesn't sound like Dougie. It sounds hard and ungiving. Cynical. Hateful.

'Your mum's not as daft as you think. She knew you'd been rummaging through your dad's old gun stuff. Asked me if we needed it for props. So I checked the prop gun. Or Alice did if I couldn't. Every single time that we practised that scene. Then, at the dress rehearsal, I knew that must be it. Lady Muck leaving her dressing-room to talk to the riffraff? No way. And sure enough there was a shiny, real bullet in the gun.'

The voice changes to a falsetto.

'Oh, officer I've no idea how that got there – but I did leave the room with the door open...'

'So I took out the real bullet and replaced it with another blank. Then I put a second blank in the gun. That's right, Stella, you shot yourself in the head with a blank from an inch or so away. Taken off a big chunk of your head, it has. Very messy. Damaged your brain. And, more importantly for you, I'll bet, your hair's ruined. It'll never grow back on this side. The police have the whole thing down as a tragic accident. Someone must have loaded two blanks... Probably you .... We've all told them how adorably absent-minded you can be ...'

Such a mean, sarcastic tone. I never knew he could be so spiteful. If I could only *speak*, I'd put paid to Mr Nasty. The police would have to drag him out in handcuffs. And I would be lying here, the wronged wife. So vulnerable. Oh, if only I could move!

'... and the doctors have tried everything but they say you're already dead. Well, if there's any justice maybe a little bit of you is still in there. I really hope so. I want you to know this.... We're going to switch off your life support and let you die. When we've buried you, I'll be the grieving widower. Just for a decent interval. Then Alice and I will play a very public falling-in-love while pursuing our mutual interest of Amateur Dramatics. This time next year we'll be married. We're hoping to start a family together and we're planning to live happily ever after. So you're not such a great actress as you think. A stint at RADA? You lasted ten weeks and if you hadn't left then, they'd have kicked you out sooner or later. Your acting fooled no-one. Alice and me, we had you sussed all along. And hey, can you hear something Stella? That's the sound of the curtain coming down!'

This can't be happening. No...no...NO! This is not the way it was supposed...

Doors

Robert hesitated at the door. He half raised a hand to knock, then let it drift back down to his side. He looked at the door. A plain white-painted wooden door... His mind drifted away from the door, just as his hand had done. There was a blank time. Then Robert noticed the door. He felt uneasy. Where did it lead to? He had found himself before it, with a sense that he needed to open it and go... somewhere. He wasn't clear about where. He thought he'd been here for a while although he wasn't sure how long. There were marks on the unfamiliar door, around the handle. Small, grubby marks like fingers. He reached out and placed his own fingertips over the marks. Wrong size. Now, what had he been about to do? He started to wander away when the handle turned, abruptly, and the door pulled open. The man who had opened it smiled brightly at him.

'There you are! What are you waiting outside for, instead of coming in? We thought you weren't hungry.'

Robert took a few unwilling steps forward, into what appeared to be a very crowded room. What was wrong with his legs? They didn't seem to be coordinating too well. He felt slow. Unsteady. His feet shuffled on soft carpet as he tried to get his bearings and make sense of where he was. The noise! He hadn't been aware of it before but now it struck him that it was very noisy in here. Chat, chat, chat.

'Chat,chat,chat.' He said it out loud.

If anything, the unknown man's smile got wider.

'Yes, that's right,' he said with a forced heartiness, 'we're all chatting while we wait for you. Let's get you sitting down before everything gets cold'.

A muddle of people around a table, about to eat. All looking at him. Smiling. The smiles seemed a little 'off'. He couldn't think why. As the stranger reached out to put an arm around him, Robert flinched away. He was suddenly very fearful. Then a voice cut across his confusion, A voice that felt like a cooling breeze on a hot summer's day. Or his mother's hand stroking his head when it ached with the 'flu. The voice was not one he could place but it calmed him.

'It's all right, Robbie, dear. Steer your dad this way. He'll be all right next to me.'

His dad... Oh. Robert looked about with interest. He hadn't seen dad in ages. Not since... As he was thinking the doorman gently took his arm and guided him to an empty seat at the table.

'This is a smart place we've come to for dinner,' he muttered, as he sat down. He turned to the elderly woman on the next chair. She seemed pleasant enough. He leaned slightly towards her and asked, in a conspiratorial whisper,

'Should I give him a tip, do you think?'

'No dear,' she said. She took his hand and patted the back of it, somewhat sadly, 'it's our Robbie. He doesn't need a tip from us. Just look at the beautiful home he's got here. You always said he'd do well, didn't you lovey?'

The hubbub around the table had subsided since his entrance and now he was aware of childish giggles.

'Dad...Dad... why does Grandad want to give you a tip?'

Several adults made shushing noises. Robert was aware of undercurrents around him. He struggled to make out any significance. Nothing made sense. Who were these people? The woman at his side was piling food onto a plate. She placed it in front of him. Then she produced a clean tea towel and carefully tied it around his neck. He tried to protest, tried to wave her arm away, but the blessed woman took no notice. She had mixed him up with somebody else. He didn't need a .... what do you call it? That thing they put on babies... He felt his mind slide sideways. He could remember times when the baby was in his pram...

***

Robert pulled the front door behind him and heard a satisfying click as it shut. He gave it a gentle push to make sure. Better safe than sorry. Then he was off down the path, through the gate, and along the road. He was trying to think what it was called. Something Street? Or Avenue? Damn, it just wouldn't come and yet he knew people who lived here. He tried to think who they were, but that information eluded him too. The road was familiar though. He felt safe just toddling along at a steady pace. There was a brief flash of memory. A hot day and a big removal van. Carol rushing around, giving instructions, producing cups of tea. Carol. He thought about the name. Decided she was someone he knew from ages back. Carol. And a sunny day. The memory left him as rapidly as it had come. He thought, it's not very sunny today. There's a chilly feeling in the air. His feet were really cold. He stopped and glanced down. His brown check slippers didn't look right, although he knew they were his. There were puddles and his feet were getting wet. An idea came to him. He should have put on those other things. The big black things you use for gardening. Or puddles. Yet again, the word he wanted eluded him. He could almost reach out and grab the words he wanted, they were *just there*. But frustratingly each word dissolved into fragments and melted away, even as his hand was about to close around it.

He reached a corner. Hesitated. Started to cross then changed his mind and retreated. Went to cross again. Backtracked. There he teetered, on the edge of the kerb, with the terror of a man facing an abyss. Everything had gone from him. His certainty about where he was, his sense of safety. He was lost in his mind. Lost in a world that made no sense. Time made no sense. He grew colder.

The bright lights blinded him, so that he had to fling an arm in front of his face. There was a terrifying roar and a voice. A man's voice. Loud. He couldn't hear properly above the roaring. The police officer signalled to his partner, who switched off the engine and came to join him.

'Not a drunk,' the first officer muttered quietly, 'it's Rob Jenner. My dad used to know him. And he used to coach the church football team when I was a lad.'

He turned to Robert and in a gentle voice said,

'Hello, Mr Jenner. What are you doing out in all this rain in your slippers? You'll catch cold if you're not careful.'

'I'm just going to the shops. I need a newspaper.'

'Not much chance of that,' said the second officer, not unkindly. 'It's the middle of the night.'

Robert looked around him. The car headlights made everything else seem even darker. It must be late. He noticed the policeman. If you want to know the time... He wasn't sure how that ended or why it had popped into his head.

'Well, nice to have met you,' he said briskly and turned. Then stopped at the edge of the kerb again as, once more, he didn't know where to go. Someone took his arm.

'We'll give you a lift, Mr Jenner,' said a cheery voice and he felt himself being turned around. He noticed the vehicle, stopped nearby.

'Ah, this must be my taxi,' he said with relief. He settled himself in the back seat and waited for the driver to start the engine. There was a brief conversation over the phone but Robert was preoccupied with a loose thread on his clothes. His fingers played with it, twisting it into the same shape, over and over. Twisting. Then letting it go. It was curiously satisfying. He hummed quietly to himself. As they pulled up outside a house, Carol opened the door. Her face was anxious, pinched-looking. She thanked the two policemen, offered a hot drink, but they had to get back on patrol.

'If you're all right, then...'

'Yes, I can sort him out now. Thank you so much. I don't know how he managed to find the key and get out.'

Robert waved goodbye to the two taxi drivers. Unusual to get two in the one cab. So kind to help him to the door - and he hadn't even paid them. He had checked his pockets but there was no money in his dressing-gown or his pyjamas. He turned and saw Carol.

'Hello dear,' he said, surprised, 'you're up late.'

***

The bedroom door opened and the woman... the one he knew... she looked after him... Robert stopped trying and lay there as she ushered in a young man. He wore a smart jacket and trousers. No tie, though. Poor show, that. Robert liked to see men dressed properly. A tie and a jacket. Always. Even when it was summer and everyone else was loosening collars and undoing buttons. Not him. He prided himself on looking his best. Robert started to cough and there was Carol by his side, holding his head still and giving him a sip of something hot and lemony.

'Look who's come to see you, love,' Carol said with a smile. 'Here's somebody you haven't seen in a long while.'

The man put down a large black case on the dressing table and turned to Robert.

'Hi, Mr Jenner. I'm sure you won't remember me. There must have been so many boys.'

'You're not a boy.' Robert frowned. He felt angry. They were trying to make him seem stupid.

'Not now,' said the man in a soothing voice, 'but years ago, when you knew me, I was a boy. You used to teach me.'

He reached into his case for a stethoscope and said down on the bed.

'I taught you to be a doctor?'

'No, no.' He laughed. 'Way before all the doctor stuff. You taught me maths and history.'

Robert considered this while the doctor listened to his chest, took his temperature.

'Maths and history,' he repeated eventually. He had another coughing fit. Then he looked the doctor in the eye and in a hoarse voice croaked,

'A lot of numbers in that.'

'Yes indeed,' the doctor considered it for a moment or two, as if Robert had said something profound, 'you're not wrong there, Mr Jenner.'

Robert leaned back on his pillow, feeling exhausted but strangely satisfied. As the doctor gathered up his things and went to leave, he looked back to say goodbye. Robert was gazing off into space, oblivious to anyone else's presence. His eyes held a flat blankness. Such a contrast to the keenly intelligent and aware man that he had known. 'What a waste,' he thought, 'I hope to god I don't have to go like that.'

***

As he came to, Robert decided he wasn't feeling too good. There was an aching pressure in his chest. And more pressure on his bladder. 'Toilet,' he mumbled, as he fought his way to the edge of the bed. He made his way to the door on shaky legs. It stood ajar and, as he paused for breath, he heard footsteps coming up the stairs. He held himself very still as he tried to think who could have got into the house. Frantically he looked around for something with which to defend himself. As the feet climbed higher a head appeared above the banister. A stranger. A burglar? Someone who had come to do him harm, of that he was convinced. The head turned and the man saw him. Said something. But Robert couldn't hear anything above the confusion raging in his head. 'Get out!' he yelled. 'Get out of my house!' The man kept on coming towards him. Robert swore, he shouted at the top of his voice, he threatened. His scratchy throat made it hard to get the words out and he frothed and spluttered obscenities at the intruder. Still the man came towards him.

'Dad,' he said, 'it's me. Robbie. Mum sent me up to help you get downstairs.'

By now his father was incoherent with fear. A wet patch spread slowly across the front of his pyjamas. Then, just as slowly, Robert's expression changed. He became very still.

'You get out of my house. You're not wanted here.' His voice was cold and harsh.

He glared at Robbie with hate-filled eyes. Then turned around and went back into the bedroom. His son took a few breaths to calm himself, before calling softly down the stairs,

'It's OK, mum. I'll check on him and get him cleaned up. You stay down there.'

He followed his father warily. Robert was sitting on the edge of the bed, wracked with coughs. A lost, crumpled, little figure. So diminished from the authoritative but loving man Robbie had known. As the coughing fit subsided he looked up, his gaze passing impassively over his son. He could have been another item of furniture in the room, for all the effect his presence had. There was no response as Robert was helped into the bathroom, gently washed, and helped into clean pyjamas. No response as he was half led, half carried down the stairs and along the hall to the kitchen.

But as Carol turned from the sink, his face was suddenly lit with the joy of recognition.

'Hello mum,' he said happily, 'I've brought my friend home for tea. Can we have beans on toast today?'

He made his way to a place at the kitchen table, while behind him his wife and son exchanged looks of despair.

***

Time shifted and swirled around without any pattern or logic. People he didn't know loomed large in his vision or shrank almost to nothing. Like looking down the wrong end of a telescope. He wasn't able to find any boundary between real things and dreams. Between memories and imaginings. Words evaded him. Concepts half formed then disappeared in a fog. He didn't feel right. His body hurt. His mind hurt. And he felt very frightened. When phrases came to him he spoke them, but no-one reacted as he wanted. They smiled or soothed. They contradicted. Then the frustration grew and he lashed out. Above all there was such a sense of loss, though what it was that had gone missing, he couldn't think. Once, as his wife held him and spooned food into his mouth, he made eye-contact. For that moment she felt she was seeing the real Robert for the first time in so long that it brought tears to her eyes.

'Don't cry,' he said in a clear, firm voice.

Then, a moment later,

'You know, there's something very wrong here.'

It was such a matter-of-fact voice. Such a recognisably-Robert voice. Even so, as she held his gaze, the person behind his eyes wandered off again, back into the fog, and he no longer knew her.

With each day that passed she found herself watching his face at every opportunity, searching for any shreds of him that remained, finding fewer and fewer glimpses of the husband who was leaving her with such painful slowness and inexorability.

***

He hadn't got over the bad chest infection of the last winter. There were regular flare-ups. By the summer he was on his third visit to the High Dependency ward, a nebuliser helping with his breathing. Carol had been told it was touch and go whether he survived this. He just didn't have any reserves of strength. She agonised over the possibility of him living almost as much as she did over the possibility of him dying. She passed most of each day by his bedside, sometimes with her son or daughter-in-law for company. Those times were easier for her. They could reminisce about the past, enjoying the memories, and hoping that, on some level, Robert could appreciate them too. But when it was just the two of them... She would try to talk to him and hope that her words might reach him. Mostly they shared a silence. Beyond words.

He was dimly aware of her hand grasping his but it seemed less real than the door that opened in his mind. It looked just like a door he knew. And when it swung noiselessly open, and he saw his sister's smiling face in the doorway, he knew he was home. The happiness bubbled up in him as he was drawn towards the doorway.

'It's wonderful to see you!' he greeted her.

He tried to think how long it had been since they had spoken but there were so many gaps inside his head. Then in a flash it came to him.

'I thought you died, Sal. But here you are, large as life!'

'Here I am,' she agreed with a laugh. 'Right as ninepence, as mum would have said.'

She looked beyond him and he turned his gaze to join hers. He could see into a cramped hospital cubicle, where machinery clicked and hummed, and numbers flickered on a continual display. A man lay in the bed, clearly not well, and Carol sat at his side. Her face was drawn and weary. She looked so desperately unhappy... And that was when he recognised himself.

'Oh Sal,' he said softly, 'have we both gone?'

'Not quite, Rob. That's up to you really. You could stay here. Or you could go back – at least for a while.'

The mist was lifting from his mind as if burned away by the hottest of sunrises. He became aware of himself for the first time in a long time.

'I can't go back to that!'

He sounded horrified at the prospect. Sal nodded thoughtfully. His eyes went again to Carol. He noticed how tightly she held onto his hand.

'It's been so hard for her. And Robbie, I guess. Maybe they would prefer it to end right now?'

His sister didn't answer at first. Then she asked,

'What has it been like for you?'

He didn't have to think too hard.

'I've been confused, angry, frustrated. But, above all, frightened.'

'What if that changed?'

'Wouldn't my mind go back to... to *that*...?' he nodded at the pitiful figure in the bed.

'Yes, but it wouldn't feel the same. It's been so awful because a part of you was still in control. A small part of you knew everything was wrong, and that was the source of the confusion and fear. Now you're at a different stage, a stage where you can just live in the moment.'

'And will that make things easier for them?'

'Oh yes, for a while they can enjoy being with you. It will be better than leaving them with thoughts of a frightened, distressed you. It will be more ...peaceful.'

She stepped back further from the door and he knew that if he chose to step with her, he would be gone from Carol and Robbie. Or he could let the door close and give them a little more time. Time to enjoy but time to accept. A gentler winding-down of what he now knew to have been a wonderful life for the most part. In the great eternal scheme what did a little unawareness matter? He realised his decision was made as soon as he felt the smoky tendrils start to invade his clear thoughts once more. He gave Sal a lopsided grin, a see-you-later wave, as he was pulled back.

***

His eyes had been open for a moment or two before Carol realised he was awake.

'Hello again, love. Look, Robbie's popped in to visit.'

Robert smiled. Such a sweet smile, she thought. She moved the nebuliser in order to give him a sip of water. Then he said, quite clearly,

'Let's pop Robbie in the pram tomorrow and take him to feed the ducks.'

'What a lovely idea!' Carol laughed.

The wrinkles smoothed from around her forehead as she relaxed a little. On the other side of the bed a grinning Robbie asked,

'And can I come too?'

Robert nodded his agreement. He couldn't put a name to the man but he had a familiar look about him. And so the three of them sat, enjoying the moment of connection while it lasted.

Wedding Cake

Marie opened her eyes. She couldn't work out where she was at first. Her feet seemed to be stuck and try as she might she couldn't wrench them free. Her neck wouldn't move, and her arms felt stiff and immobile, trapped against her sides. Ahead of her was an expanse of white. Snow? Was she outside in the snow? It didn't feel cold. She had no recollection of how she had got here. Fear struck her. Were they skiing somewhere? And had she had an accident? Oh god, maybe she'd been paralysed. Her heart pounded in her chest. But wait, she was upright. That made no sense. The last thing she remembered was the row with Nick, just before they'd gone to bed. Think! Think! It wasn't their bed, that's it, it was the hotel. They were at the hotel. Nick had stayed down in the bar – far too late – and had come in drunk and ready for a fight. That was when they had really let rip. Told each other exactly what they thought. And then some. Each of them trying to wound the other, and each of them knowing the best, most sensitive, places to hit. She tried again to move. Nothing happened. Her eyes strained to see more, to work out where she was and what was happening. Then she became aware of a figure to her side. She rolled her eyes to her right, straining to see.

Nick. But ... not Nick, somehow. He stood there, shoulder to shoulder with her, almost touching, sporting a smart black suit, a top hat, a flower in his button-hole. His eyes were swung her way and she could see a terrified, desperate look to them. His face showed no other emotion. It was sort of plasticky and unreal-looking. As was the rest of him. He didn't move. He didn't speak. He seemed to be in the same stuck state as her. The light was dim so it was hard to make out details but her eyes flicked around, trying to see, to understand, and she thought he was able to pick up on her confusion. She tried to indicate with her eyes.. what? where? how? He seemed to be just as confused. Or was she reading more into his eyes than was there?

There was a loud click and lights came on overhead. At first the glare was too much but as her eyes adjusted she could see that the snow ended in some rather fancy swirls. And that the edge was circular. There were flowers placed at intervals along this edge, cream-coloured orchids. It was like a giant wedding cake! Beyond was a cavernous space filled with enormous chairs and tables, set for a wedding breakfast. Festoons of silky material. Flowers, horseshoes, fairy-lights. It was just the wedding party they had planned, she and Katy.

Katy. That was it. They were at the hotel for the wedding. Katy was marrying Steve tomorrow. Well, today if she had woken up, but she rather suspected she was still asleep and dreaming. With a sudden dizzying realisation she understood that the furniture wasn't huge but that, in this dream world, she was very small. She and Nick, side by side, on a wedding cake. Like the little figures of the bride and groom. Hells' bells. No wonder poor Nick looked so plasticky. She might have giggled if she'd been able to, then realised that she must be plasticky too. Well, what a weird dream. She waited to wake up.

Some time later caterers appeared in the hall, adjusting settings, polishing glasses. There seemed to be a woman in charge directing everything. At one point she came quite close to the table with the cake, and Marie recognised her as Emma from Wedding Feasts, the caterers they were paying for. This was an incredibly detailed dream. Although she recognised Emma now, she would have been hard-pressed to describe her to someone. It was as though her subconscious had stored a photographic description and now, in a dreaming state, her mind had been able to retrieve it and construct an accurate image. Amazing! Still she waited to wake up.

There was a clock on the far wall and by screwing up her eyes she was able to make out the time as 2.15. The wedding was planned for 1.30 the next day and the guests were due to arrive in the hall at about 2.30. How interesting. Would her dream continue to construct the events as they were planned to happen? In that case, she would be able to see herself arriving. The clock continued to move slowly forward. She could see it moving and experience each second. That had never happened in a dream before. There wasn't usually a sense of time passing just as in real life. It tended to jump about. She glanced again at Nick. He, too, had his gaze fixed on the hands of the clock but he seemed to sense her looking and swivelled his eyes. Again she had the sensation that he was panicked and distressed. Could you really read that much into someone's eyes? Even someone you'd spent nearly thirty years with?

Like a bucket of cold water emptying over her, she remembered the row they'd had before bed and looked away from him. Things had been bad for such a long time. In secret she'd nursed the thought that once Katy was married they could split up. Get divorced. Start over. It had seemed as though their daughter was the only glue holding their relationship together. She hadn't realised Nick had been thinking the same way. Not until last night.

'... and I want a divorce, you hear me?'

'*You* want a divorce? Well, that makes two of us. I'm sick of you. And I'm sick of this.'

'You think I'm happy? I can't remember the last time I actually looked forward to coming home.'

By now they were both shouting.

'And I can't remember the last time I looked forward to you coming home!'

She had burst into tears. He had slammed into the bathroom. Thank god they'd booked a twin room, not a double. By the time he emerged the lights were out and she was under the covers feigning sleep. He'd stumbled around in the dark, in the unfamiliar room, cursing under his breath. Seconds later, it seemed, he was snoring loud enough to wake the dead while she lay there tossing and turning, and sending hateful thoughts across the gulf between them.

Their marriage was over. And soon this dream would be over too. She would wake up, paint on a happy face for their daughter's sake and play the part of proud parent. Just for today they would have to be civil to each other. Make it look as though they were having a wonderful time. It was a miserable thought. She could remember every detail of their own wedding day, and how happy they had been. She had always thought they would grow old together, mellow into one of those lovely couples you would see sometimes. In their seventies or eighties, yet still walking along arm in arm or holding hands. It always brought a lump to her throat and she'd wonder how many years they had seen in, and out, together. How many difficulties they'd faced together. United. If only Nick had stayed the same sweet, loving, funny man she had known.

The servers were suddenly standing still, looking towards the doors. Shocked, she noticed that the clock had moved on. It was just after half past. The double doors were opened and in walked Katy and Steve. Oh, they looked so happy. Katy was radiant. But why was she still dreaming? Surely it was time to wake up now. She willed herself to wake. To drop out of this mad dream. Katy and her new husband continued across the carpeted floor, the bridal party following. And there they were – the bride's parents. Walking with Steve's parents, chatting and laughing together. Pat and Richard Boyland were very animated. She and Nick somewhat less so. If anything they looked rather stiff and rigid. Shiny-faced. Unreal. They were wearing the right outfits but the clothes were in some way part of them. Now she realised the two of them were like giant plastic wedding cake ornaments. Surely the rest of the guests could see that they weren't right? But no, everyone took their places and once the happy couple were seated they all sat too.

The awful dream continued. There was the dinner they had planned and Nick had paid for. The guests apparently enjoyed it. People were laughing, taking impromptu snaps of the proceedings, drinking champagne. Then came the speeches. Plastic Nick stood up as father of the bride and began thanking everyone for coming. It sounded exactly like Nick's voice but it was strange issuing forth from a mouth that barely moved. He welcomed Steve to the family, talked about his hopes that the Boylands and the Pritchards would share many more family occasions, said what a wonderful daughter Katy had been. Then, with a slight huskiness in his voice, he turned to Plastic Marie.

'Before I finish I just want to pay tribute to Katy's mother, my beautiful wife Marie. Like the rest of you we've had our ups and down but we've always got through them together.' He paused as heads nodded in recognition. 'We vowed on our wedding day to support and love and care for each other, and that is what we've done. I can only wish that Katy and Steve enjoy the same sort of marriage. You know,' he turned towards the couple, 'the secret is to marry the perfect partner. That's what we did, and I think it's what you've done too.' He raised his glass and toasted them.

The guests clapped appreciatively and then Plastic Nick sat down. As he did Marie noticed that her counterpart rested a hand on his arm, while the two of them shared a private smile. Next Steve's friend bumbled his way through the best man's speech but it was taken in good part by everybody and was, at least, mercifully short. The bridesmaids were thanked. More toasts were drunk. Finally there came the cutting of the cake. Marie couldn't see a thing with the newly-weds standing behind her, just the flashes of cameras as all the guests tried to capture the scene. The plastic parents stood to one side, arms stiffly linked. Then as everyone turned to go back to their seats and wait for the cake to be brought around, the two turned their plastic heads towards the couple on the cake. Plastic Marie mouthed something. Then they joined the others.

In spite of the stiff face and barely moving lips, Marie had no trouble working out what the message was. 'Mine!' But what was she referring to? Nick? Their marriage? Maybe both. A large part of Marie's life. A part which, just hours ago, she had thought of as being awful. Unwanted. Something to be discarded. Just then the cake was wheeled away on its special trolley table, out to the kitchen area, to be cut into slices. The plastic figures were unceremoniously put to one side. Marie found herself lying face to face with Nick. His eyes were the only part of him that seemed alive. Oh, if only she could tell him how sorry she was. Plastic Nick had been right about their marriage. It was only lately they'd drifted apart. Surely it wasn't too late to put things right? A tiny plasticky tear slowly made its way from the corner of one eye. Her sight misted over. Nick became a blurry heap in front of her. A blurry heap that resolved into a bedside table just inches from her face.

Marie rolled over and sat bolt upright in the bed, her heart racing, sweat on her forehead. Disorientated, she looked around the room. The hotel. Of course. Oh, the relief at having woken from the dream. She looked round. Nick, too, was just struggling awake.

'Well,' she said, trying to keep her voice light, 'today's the day.'

'Yes,' Nick replied.

There was a pause then both of them spoke.

'Look I'm really sorry...'

'I'm sorry about last...'

Another pause. Then Marie suggested, tentatively,

'Maybe after the wedding's over we could sit and talk things through? We've been a bit off-kilter lately, what with all the wedding plans.'

Nick seized upon the idea.

'Great, but for now let's just enjoy our daughter's special day!'

They smiled at each other, both hugely relieved. Then got on with their preparations.

It was later, while she was checking with the caterers, that she caught herself staring at the wedding cake. The plastic couple stood there, ramrod stiff. Their features nothing like those of Marie or Nick. All the same she felt uneasy about them. So she telephoned through to Katy's room and told her there was a slight hitch with the cake. Nothing to worry about. It was just that the plastic figures looked a bit tacky. Could she replace them with a spray of orchids? That was fine by Katy so the couple were slipped into Marie's handbag and taken back to the room. Nick was ready to go and turned from the mirror just as she took them out and stood them on the bedside table. His face went pale.

'Nick, are you okay?'

'Fine,' he told her a little shakily. 'But I think you were right about me overdoing the drinking last night. I had the weirdest dream…'

And God Laughed

The endless Nothing was all. Until God thought of Something. There was no name for what that Something might be but it flickered in the sight God had now acquired. More flickers all around, lighting the darkness. God was entranced by their beauty. Each flicker took eons to form, to grow, to shrink, to fade, but to God the dance of the stars was like a pulse throbbing. There was pattern to their movement, to their ebb and flow, and for many cycles of their lifetimes they were enough. God felt their heat against the piercing cold of the dark. A little push of thought and energy was all it took for another star to take its place. As each star died, a gentle flow of energy returned and with it the knowledge of its existence apart. God was a star, a constellation, a galaxy, the universe – God was All Words. And the words that were created with the stars were fire and water, rock and gas. Every star with its own words created a new story. But in time the stories of the stars – each one different, yet each one the same – led to a new thought. Could there be something Else?

And with the thought there came existence. An existence that was not star. In the turmoil of its beginning each star threw off chunks of itself, sizzling and burning in the coldness of the space between. As these cooled they became separate. They took on a different aspect depending upon the elements and gases of which they were composed. And on some of these, new forms arose. They were not star or rock but became softer forms. They were not fixed in the heavenly dance of their progenitors but created new and infinitely more complex dances.

After a while some of these life-forms faded away, carrying the energy memory of their consciousness to God's awareness. Others changed and evolved until on some planets there were many different versions of energy. And on one planet in particular the combination of elements gave rise to an explosion of different life-forms. They moved on land, in water, through the air. They writhed and dug, crawled and galloped. It was a frenzy of movement. It caught God's attention but by watching so intently an unspoken thought sent a tiny extra spark of God's awareness towards the life-forms. And some became aware of themselves.

They knew themselves and each other, but as separate beings. They did not understand what they were and the wonderfulness of their lives. They only knew their separateness, their aloneness. This was a sad thing and God pondered how best to reconnect with them. But trying to make them aware of God energy was not easy. Their thoughts were not attuned to the dance of life and they misunderstood so easily. God watched as they made sense of their existence by inventing gods. These were not part of the energy that created life, that was life, but merely claimed power over it. They were not real, just the imaginings of many minds, all working separately. These imagined gods were cruel and harsh, acting on whims, demanding or dictating how life should be lived. God, who wanted nothing more than for life to be as it chose to be, could only wait to see if one day people would know the truth about themselves.

The imagined gods became a tool to be used by some people against others. They gave the right to be held up as more important, of greater worth. They took away the right to self-determination and the freedom to choose. Sometimes they inspired great goodness in people, encouraging them to give their lives in the service of others. More often they inspired war and hatred. They set person against person. Nation against nation. When the people lived without awareness of their connection, of their godness, they created rules to define their place in creation. They made a world of 'them' and 'us'. And all of them believed their version of the truth to be the absolute truth, rejecting the views of others as wrong, misguided, or a terrible thing that should be rooted out by force.

As each person's life ended their energy returned and God was completed by them again, just as they now knew themselves as God. But while each one lived there was no connection. So it was possible to enjoy a life of comfort while others starved for lack of food, froze for lack of shelter, suffered needlessly for lack of care. It was possible to hurt or even kill others, because they were 'other' and not 'self'.

Some in their search for meaning found a tiny spark of God's original thought, hidden within them. Every cell, every atom, every particle of their being was bound up with the joy and wonder of creation. And everything came from the energy of God-thought. They glimpsed the truth and tried to live their lives accordingly. And finally, after many generations, these views began to hold sway. More and more people realised the godness of existence. God watched the process without interfering and wondered what would be next.

Meanwhile the stars still continued in the heavens in the patterns created for them. They too were of God and carried the original thought in themselves. Until one day it moved them into a dance of change and evolution. Their influence combined with that of the many who longed for a world of peace and harmony. The wheel of the heavens turned and all the people began to see themselves and others as the truth within them.

The planet upon which they lived became a world of sharing and communion. They joined together to create a world in which want and greed, hatred and anger were strangers. There was such joy in their living, but even greater joy in their not-living for now they knew this not as an ending but a returning. Finally their evolution was such that none could see further reason for delaying their return.

Once again there was Nothing. And for countless ages the Nothing was all. But unlike before God was aware. Slowly God remembered. Every moment of life, every thought, every deed. All the sorrows and the many joys. Within God was the knowledge of all that had been created and experienced. Such richness of existence. What else might have been? What else might still be?

Thought was Creation. And Creation was Wonderful. And so God laughed for the joy of it all. And as the laugh, too deep for sound, vibrated across the Nothing it left in its wake the first few stars, twinkling into existence.

Made in the USA
Charleston, SC
14 March 2016